One Hot Summer in Kyoto

Kazumi is well-acquainted with the shopkeepers, who now know me, and I sense that my being with her solves the riddle that has been in their minds. The woman in the butcher's shop seems to give me a knowing look, as if to say, "Now I understand why you have come to spend the hot summer in Kyoto," and the young man in the grocer's eyes me quizzically, says something to the girl assistant who glances in my direction, and sniggers. Such is my impression, but I may well be wrong; it is easy for a foreigner to misinterpret a Japanese regard,

a Japanese smile.

ONE HOT SUMMER IN KYOTO

John Haylock

STONE BRIDGE PRESS • Berkeley, California

The translations from the T'ang poet Li Ho are from *The Chinese Conception of Poetry* by Professor Naotaro Kudo of Waseda University, Tokyo.

The dialogue from the Kabuki play *Kagotsurube* is from *Six Kabuki Plays*, translated by Donald Richie and Miyoko Watanabe (Tokyo: Hokuseido Press, 1963).

Published by STONE BRIDGE PRESS
P.O. Box 8208, Berkeley, CA 94707

Originally published in the United Kingdom
by London Magazine Editions in 1980.

FIRST U.S. EDITION, 1993.

Cover design by Studio Silicon.

Text design by Peter Goodman.

10 9 8 7 6 5 4 3 2 1

Library of Congress Catalog Card Number: 93- 85075
ISBN 1-880656-08-6

to Hiro Asami

1 Although I have done this journey from Tokyo to Kyoto many times and know there is still plenty of time, I obey the warning of the train's imminent arrival and "assemble my luggage and get ready to alight," as the official female voice advises in English after the longer Japanese announcement. I wait in the aisle wedged in by my two suitcases and those of other alighting passengers. The super-express slows gently and comes to a halt. There is a pressing forward. Passing from the air-conditioned carriage to the sweltering platform is like going into a hot conservatory from a wintry garden.

The house I have rented for July and August is in a lane off a wide road that leads past the great *torii* of the Heian Shrine and goes to the foot of a steep hill which is covered with pines and maples; at its base are the buildings of Nanzenji temple; the lane, "my" lane, is asphalted and just wide enough for the taxi, but the driver doesn't want to enter it, so he stops at its entrance. He helps me, somewhat reluctantly as Japanese taxi drivers don't like carrying bags, with my luggage, placing the suitcase he is holding in the middle of the lane only half way to the house, the first on the right after a roofed garden wall and only thirty paces from the corner. I pay the driver, get out the key which the landlord, an American who is vacationing in California, sent me by registered post, and unlock the fragile, sliding door of opaque glass panels. The door is rickety and the catch could easily be broken by a determined child; the other houses in the lane look equally unsubstantial; some like mine have two stories, others only one.

I take off my shoes in the doll's-house porch in which there is a small chest of drawers. On this piece of furniture is a vase containing three red gladioli and above it hangs a wooden theatrical mask of a smiling old man with a wispy white beard. I push open two flimsy wood and paper doors and step up into a matted hall—hall is hardly the right word since it is a space of about two square yards—and I am confronted and flanked by sliding fusuma screens. I pause to choose—it is like a problem in a party game. The fusuma on my left reveals a flight of precipitous stairs that are not at all inviting on this torrid afternoon; the two fusuma facing me form one wall of a murky little sitting room and the two on the right screen a dining recess. In the recess is an eighteen-inch-high lacquer table over a hole resembling a garage inspection pit. These holes enable lovers of old Japanese habits to cheat: they sit on the floor, yes, but with their legs dangling instead of folded under them in excruciating discomfort. Some advanced Japanophiles protest that they like sitting on their heels, but I wonder if they really enjoy doing so. I am glad that my landlord doesn't, for I hate sitting on the floor without any support for my back. There is a sliding door between the recess and the kitchen. Except for a picture window that looks on an umbragious garden of rocks, shrubs, and trees, the walls of the sitting room consist of sliding doors; on one wall, however, there is just enough space for an abstract painting: blobs of crimson on a gray background.

I slide open the doors opposite the window and nearly bump my nose on a television set above which is an air conditioner. I turn on the latter but it doesn't work; the former does. It is very hot in this little room of doors and I don't much care for television. On a table between the two bench seats that make up the Western-style furniture is a vase of white chrysanthemums. I remember the gladioli in the *genkan* (the porch-entryway) and wonder how these flowers have kept alive, for I know my landlord left over a week ago. The vase is full of water. The daily maid must have put them there.

I open the one sliding door that remains to be opened and I find myself in a dark passage: on the left is the bathroom, a narrow room that contains in a row a hand basin, a lavatory (sit-down type, thank heavens!), a shower, and, at the end by the window, a deep Japanese wooden tub. I fumble about the passage and push open yet another sliding door and discover a room in Japanese style with matted floor and no furniture. There is a pile of five cushions and in the *tokonoma* are a pottery vase with no flowers in it and a scroll of calligraphy. One side of the room consists of two paper-paneled sliding doors that screen sliding windows which give on to another part of the garden and the main house—"my" house is only a subsidiary building on the property. Though very hot and stuffy this room is charming and is, I conjecture, a moon-viewing room. I don't think that I shall be using it much, not that there won't be a moon to view, but it would mean sitting on the floor.

Outside this room there is another precipitous staircase which I climb on all fours. In the room above the moon-viewing room I find evidence of female occupation. A futon is laid out on the tatami with sheets and a small pillow; the top sheet is rolled back and the bottom sheet is no longer tucked under the futon. It looks as if someone got up in a hurry and didn't have time to roll up the futon or fold the sheets; also, there are clothes, underclothes, and blouses on the floor, screwed up, unwashed; and other clothes hang from hangers hooked on to the ledge above the window. In the room there is a smell, a smell of perfume and of a woman. Who is she? A caretaker about whom I have not been informed? I am disconcerted and curious, outraged and expectant. I was told that the maid was a daily.

I descend the ladder-like stairs backwards and cross the house to the other staircase, which I mount with caution. The bedroom at the top, although matted, has Western comforts: a double bed, a bedside table with a reading lamp, a chest of drawers, a cupboard for clothes, a desk with an angle-poise lamp, book shelves, two basket armchairs, and two large windows. One window looks into the garden of the main house and the gray-tiled roof of an outhouse, and the other, which faces the little street, looks across to a temple compound planted with pines and poplars and the veranda entrance of the principal building, the roof of which sweeps gently downwards to turn upwards at the corners in graceful curves.

I lug my suitcases up the stairs and unpack in the gale of an electric fan. It is a leaden day and the air is heavy and humid. And then, still feeling an interloper, I examine the kitchen. I am delighted to find that this important room in the house is well equipped and contains an interesting collection of cookery books including *Larousse Gastronomique* and *Cuisines et Vins de France* by Curnowsky, Prince élu des Gastronomes (1927). I take these two tomes upstairs and peruse them. The colored photographs of the *oie aux marrons* and *chapon du maitre Raymond* make my mouth water and I quite forget that I lunched in the buffet car on the train, albeit badly, when I read on of the suggested *menus d'été*. What shall I do about dinner? Go out? I doze off with the book of the Prince élu des Gastronomes open at a picture of *carée de porc en bellevue*, which looks tempting and succulent, wondering whether the lady of the upper moon-viewing room can cook.

2 When I awake my neck and back are sticky with sweat. I put a towel round what was once my waist (since giving up smoking my stomach has swollen disastrously) and go down the dangerous stairs sideways, one step at a time, with my hands clinging to the walls in the manner of an amateur mountaineer descending a smooth rock face. A whiff of scent pervades the sitting room. "She" has obviously just passed through the house and gone up the other stairs to her room. I have a quick shower, mount "my" stairs again, put on a shirt and a pair of slacks, and then make the perilous descent. If there were a fire I am sure I would break my leg trying to hurry out of the house.

"Good evening!" I cry into the dark passage on the other side of the sitting room. "Good evening!"

There comes an "oh!"—not an English "oh!" but a sudden guttural one of surprise, almost a gasp; movement follows, the pad of feet, and finally the appearance in the sitting room of a Japanese woman of about—ages are difficult to judge—thirty? Her face is slightly wrinkled at the eyes and on the forehead; that she is mature is the first thing I notice about her.

"Mr. Meadowes?"

"Yes, you are?"

"Kazumi Kato." Her dark brown eyes twinkle; her red lips part revealing good, regular teeth, one of which, a side one, is gold. "Mr. Simpson told you about me?"

"No."

She laughs nervously. "He so busy before he left for the States." Her accent is American. "He must forget to say he ask me to look after till you come, and to show you everything."

"You speak such good English."

"No, I don't. My English is very bad."

"There's one thing . . ."

"Yes?"

"How do you turn on the air conditioner? I tried and—"

"I show you."

I join her by the machine and as she stretches up into the cupboard to connect the main switch her hair touches my cheek.

"I could never have found that."

The machine begins to eject a cool blast.

"That's better," I say with feeling.

"Would you like me to show you kitchen?"

She is like an efficient housekeeper.

"Let's sit in the cool for a bit. It's terribly hot outside this little room."

"Your fan in your bedroom, you can work?"

"Yes, thanks."

We lapse into silence. I take surreptitious glances at her profile which, for a Japanese, is good—I realize it's insulting to say "for a Japanese," but what else can one say when most faces in this land are flat? Her nose turns up slightly and her nostrils are more elongated than is usual. Noriko's nostrils are like little round holes in cheese. My wife's? Trying to recall my wife's nostrils, I look out of the picture window at a shrub and the lower half of a tree with short branches and big leaves. A brown leaf flutters to the ground.

"Premature," I say.

"Pardon?"

"A reminder that autumn will come."

"That tree paulownia tree. We make, chests and *geta*, the wooden clogs, from paulownia wood."

She evidently doesn't know that I've been five years in Japan. "*Kiri* in Japanese, isn't it?"

"Ah, you speak Japanese?"

"Only a few words."

"I think more."

"No, really." The fact is I don't. I know enough to fool a foreigner, that is all.

After a long two minutes, Kazumi says, "Maybe you now feel enough cool?"

"Yes, thanks."

"You like to see kitchen?"

I nod.

She shows me the stove, the pots, the pans, the cupboards, and while indicating the jars that contain rice, sugar, and so on, she notices that the two cookery books are missing. "Two books not here."

"I took them upstairs to read."

"Oh, I see." She seems displeased.

"You know where everything is in this house."

"I live here."

"I didn't know."

"I mean I do not live here now. Before I live here."

I go into the sitting room and lower myself onto the bench seat against the window, making the pane rattle, as it would in an earth tremor.

"You do not mind?"

I raise my eyebrows.

"You do not mind I look after the house while?"

"On the contrary, I am grateful to you." I jerk a nod-bow, an infectious gesture caught from the Japanese. "Thank you very much."

"*Do itashimashite.*"

A pause.

"Don't you have a wife?"

"Yes, but she is in England looking after our daughter."

"You have Japanese girlfriend?"

This is so unexpected that I answer truthfully, "Yes, in Tokyo." I do not add that I am tired of Noriko.

"*Aa, so desu ka?*" An oft-repeated expression meaning "Is that so?" This is said with respect, for one has to be rich to maintain a mistress in Japan unless you are clever like me and run one on the cheap, exploiting the fact that she is genuinely in love. In any case, I am rich, fairly (or used to be, for who is rich today?)—not as rich as my wife, though, whose financial independence has often irritated me.

"You are English, then?" This is asked with a certain amount of surprise as most Japanese assume that foreigners are American. "You like some tea?"

"I'd rather have whiskey."

"I don't know if Simpson-san he left any—"

"I wouldn't dream of drinking his. I brought a bottle with me. It's upstairs." I rise.

"I get it."

"No, you get some ice."

"Okay."

When I return to the sitting room she is still in the kitchen, but in a few minutes she appears with a tray bearing a plastic ice bucket, two glasses with protective little socks round their bases, a jug of water, and a plate on which slices of processed cheese and canned pressed beef have been arranged in a neat circle.

"Chivas Regal," she says with respect, after glancing at my bottle.

"A duty-free bottle. Like some?"

"Yes, please."

Her eagerness surprises me for Japanese women do not usually drink; perhaps she has learned foreign habits from Simpson. I imagine that she does not come from a very high class family; bar-hostess stratum probably, but there is nothing wrong with that. She kneels in the manner of a Japanese wife and administers unto me. All very nice.

"Do you know Mr. Watkins? I must look him up." I say this to make conversation. I am not in the least hurry to see him.

"Simpson-san know him well. I know him a little. You want I telephone Professor Watkins?"

"No, later. What about dinner? Would you like to eat with me?" She looks down.

"I invite you out to dinner. Where shall we go?"

"Thank you very much. I must go my *apato*."

"No need to do that." The whiskey encourages me. "Why not spend the night? There are all sorts of questions I want to ask you: about milk, newspaper delivery, where the butcher and the baker are, the shops."

"Simpson-san he buy most things in the market. It is—"
"Show me tomorrow. Let's go and eat."

3 At a Western-style restaurant in the vicinity we dine on what is called Wiener Schnitzel but is in fact only a travesty of that dish, and then we return to the house. The air-conditioned room, I now realize, with all its sliding doors, resembles a waiting-room, an ante-room, and long occupation of it would make one restless; the bench seats are narrow and although they have backs and springs they are not comfortable. We sit: I on one bench seat and Kazumi on the other. I feel we are patients awaiting our turn and that we should be flipping over the pages of glossy magazines. Our conversation is desultory.

"What is the name of the temple opposite?" I ask.
"I don't know. I am sorry."
"What sect does it belong to?"
"I am sorry. I don't know."

The silence into which we lapse is interrupted by the telephone. Kazumi jumps up, goes to the dining recess, kneels, and picks up the instrument which is kept on the floor in a corner.

"It is for you from Tokyo." She rises in one easy, graceful movement and I take the receiver from her. I bend over the phone as the wire is short. It is Noriko, my mistress.

"Who is *she?*" Noriko asks, peremptorily.
"Wait a moment." I squat on the floor.
"Who is *she?*"
"I'll tell you later."
"Who is *she?*"

It is difficult to explain with Kazumi sitting three yards away. "I'll tell you later."

"Who is *she?*"
"Friend."
"Your friend?"

"My friend's friend." I stretch out my legs.

"Why is she there?"

"Showing me the place."

"I see," says Noriko, suspiciously.

I lie flat on my back with my head in the sitting room. Kazumi is staring at me.

"Will she stay there with you?"

"Of course not."

"I think she may stay."

"Does it matter?"

"Yes, does it matter." Noriko has always made this mistake.

I try to change the subject. "Thank you for coming to see me off at the station this morning."

Noriko came to Tokyo Station to say goodbye this morning. She didn't bow like some other Japanese on the platform who were seeing off a senior member of their company, she just looked sad and anxious. This made me feel guilty. I always feel guilty when I leave Noriko and yet when I am with her I am bored and often long to get away.

She continues, "Will that person stay in the house with you?"

"No."

"Where will she go?"

"I don't know. I'll explain in a letter. When will you come down?" Feeling contrite about leaving her for two months, I asked Noriko to come and stay in Kyoto for a few days during the summer.

"Soon, I think."

"Let me know in good time." I don't want any surprise arrival.

There is a pause which is disconcerting as it is a long-distance call.

"I'll write," I say. "Goodbye for now."

I ring off.

I roll over on my stomach, replace the receiver and crawl to the bench seat against which I lean.

"That was your girlfriend?"

"Yes."

"She ask about me?"

"Yes."

The fact that one takes off one's shoes in a Japanese house produces a feeling of informality, at least it makes one feel informal and promotes the possibility of making informal moves. "Footsie" is a game played with more subtlety in Japan than in those lands where feet remain shod most of the time; it is easy to press one's toes inadvertently-on-purpose against the stockinged foot of another person and for the gesture to be as vague as a Japanese answer to a direct question. I push my right foot slowly forward and touch Kazumi's instep. She does not move her foot. I apply pressure. I gently rub my big toe up and down. Her foot remains stationary.

"What did she say?" inquires Kazumi, after a few moments of instep rubbing.

"Who?"

"Your girlfriend." She withdraws her foot, but naturally, for she shifts slightly in her seat. I do not take the movement as a rebuff.

"She was surprised that you answered the phone."

"Jealous?"

"I suppose so." I push my foot forward and touch hers again. "I don't care."

Kazumi gets up and switches on the television set. A panel game is in progress. The panel of four judges has to guess which of three sets of identically dressed people is the singer, the pet-bird keeper, or the folk dancer. The Japanese is too fast for me to follow so I ask Kazumi to translate; she does, but perfunctorily; she seems to have a deep interest in the game and concentrates on it as if it were important. She is no intellectual.

While she gazes at the screen I gaze at her—she is too absorbed to notice that my eyes are scrutinizing her face. I admire her nose that turns up at the end (I dislike turned-down noses; my wife's nose turns down); it is a little nose, being a Japanese one, but it has character, as does her forehead, which is high and therefore rather contradicts her partiality for TV guessing games. Her hair, black of course, is neatly waved and a few strands fall over her forehead making a slight fringe; her eyebrows have been weeded rather than plucked for they are fairly thick, but they are tidy and form perfect arcs. Her mouth is well shaped. It goes without saying that her eyes are dark, but Japanese eyes vary within their small range from very dark brown, almost black, to hazel. Kazumi's eyes are chestnut. But features mentioned singly mean little; dissecting a face and describing its parts is as pointless as pulling an orchid to bits—"'tis not a lip or eye we beauty call, but the joint force and full result of all." And the "joint force" and "full result" of Kazumi's face is pleasing. I find her attractive in a Japanese way, but then I like Mongolian features more than Western ones.

I renew my game of footsie but this time Kazumi removes her toe to the other side of the occasional table, a converted wooden charcoal brazier, heavy as a boulder—what Japanophile aesthetes will go through to show their preference for things indigenous!

The wretched quiz game ends.

"You like call Professor Watkins?"

"I'll call him tomorrow."

Watkins is an American. He has lived in Kyoto for many years and is married to a Japanese whom he keeps firmly under control in the manner of husbands of this country—at least that is what everyone says. I like him, although I don't know him very well; I am not in the mood, though, to see him at the moment. I am sure he will want to tell me about the drama festival he helps to organize and I don't want to hear about it, not tonight anyway.

Kazumi switches to another TV station. Commercials are on and when at last they are over she becomes absorbed again in a dubbed Western. It is funny to hear cowboy-hatted, horse-riding, pistol-twirling Americans speaking fluent Japanese.

I want to ask her if she is going home tonight or not, but I fear that if I do pose the question she will take it to mean I want her to go, and I don't. I want her to stay. One has to be careful; it is easy to upset someone unintentionally; even after five years I am always saying the wrong thing. The language is the trouble: English is so direct in comparison with Japanese, and therefore what would seem to a Westerner an innocuous remark bereft of any innuendo might be interpreted by a Japanese as being heavy with hints; so should I say anything slightly connected with the immediate future she might assume that I desired to send her packing.

I watch all the Western; I sit through a talk, a Japanese domestic drama in which the characters seem to behave very hysterically, a recital of Japanese songs sung alternately by men and women in kimono, the news, and a commentary on the news. This takes us until after eleven. The commercials increase. A sex show starts: a scantily dressed blonde winding a python erotically round herself. Kazumi seems to like this. I don't. I hate striptease and the drooling it is meant to incite. I get up. She at once rises and turns off the television.

"No, don't move," I say. "I didn't mean to disturb you. Please go on watching the—"

"It is late. You must be tired. I am sorry."

"There is nothing to be sorry about."

"It is a little late to go to my *apato*."

"You mustn't dream of going to your *apato*. You must stay here." Do I sound too eager?

"Simpson-san he say maybe you like me stay few days so as you say before I show you—"

"Stay as long as you please."

"Thank you. It is very kind of you."

Our politenesses continue for a little longer until I break them off by going into the bathroom to clean my teeth. When I get up to the bedroom, Kazumi is standing by the bedside table lighting a green coil, an anti-mosquito device that lets off a pleasant aroma.

Kazumi says, "I light *katori senko*."

"Thank you very much. But is it necessary? The windows are screened."

"Maybe some mosquitoes come in." She bends over the ashtray to see if the coil is burning properly; this action is redundant as I can see from the other side of the room that it is well alight; such fussing is typical. But in this case does it have a meaning? Is it a signal? I go down the gap between the bed and the window (she is still bending over the coil), put my hands on her tiny waist. She twists her head and my lips land on her cheek.

"No," she says.

"Why?"

"I am sorry."

I am blocking the way so she jumps on the bed and then off the other side. "Goodni'," she cries, and runs down the ladder stairs with the agility of an acrobat. I do not give chase.

The fan blows the fragrance of the *katori senko* into my face as I lie in bed thinking of Kazumi. I tell myself that the best thing has happened, for once one has been to bed with a woman and whispered all those meaningless terms of endearment she has you trapped. I have come to Kyoto to get out of a trap. Nevertheless, my pride has been slightly wounded.

The trap I have come here to get out of is Noriko. Fortunately she has a job in Tokyo and is not able to travel. Perhaps meanly, I have never given her much money; perhaps wisely, I have never allowed her to live with me; perhaps cruelly, in the last year or so I have usually only let her see me once a week. Saturday has been our day. Often I have not met her till six in the evening and sometimes on Sunday I have invented a luncheon engagement which has meant she has had to be out of my flat by eleven o'clock. The trouble is that she has not minded all this; and more, she has never objected to the fact that I am married and that because of my child I am unwilling to divorce my wife. Noriko is content to be my mistress, it seems; or possibly she may regard herself as my Number-Two wife, a status that is recognized in Japan. My Number-One wife, my English wife, would never have accepted Noriko and so I deceive her or think I do; there is a chance that she guesses, but she has not mentioned anything. Our daughter is of elementary school age, and my wife and I agreed that she should be educated in England; in any case Monica detests Japan and prefers living in our house in Suffolk.

My decision to spend the two-months' holiday in Japan has not been challenged by my wife; she has got to the state, I think, whereby she doesn't much care what I do or where I am; divorce, though, we have never seriously discussed. At the moment we seem to be going our own ways, occasionally corresponding. I have purposely not given her my address in Kyoto, simply saying that I'd be traveling about during July and August. I have come here to escape, to be out of touch—it was impossible, though, not to give Noriko my telephone number. I chose Kyoto for this interval of freedom because I infinitely prefer it to any other city in Japan and to most in the world.

Wooden clappers start to clack in the temple. Their loud tapping pierces the night. A priest must be saying a sutra.

4

The heat prevented me from drawing the curtains in the bedroom so the light wakes me at five. The sun, however, does not enter the room as the windows face south and west. From my bed I can see the gray tiles of the roof of a subsidiary building in the temple courtyard, the roof of the outhouse in the garden of this house behind which rise a palm, a ginkgo tree, and a maple—the paulownia tree is not in view. The ridge of the outhouse roof finishes with an elegantly shaped end-tile composed of three curls like a snake, the middle curl being higher than the other two.

I gaze out of the window and muse, enjoying the cool which will not last. Then I doze off again and do not stir until the metallic click of the refrigerator doors awakens me. It is eight-fifteen according to the electric digital bedside clock. Kazumi must be up.

It is inconvenient that the bathroom and the lavatory are on the ground floor, for now that Kazumi is up I shall have to put on some respectable garment when I descend. I put on my *yukata*, rather a hot piece of clothing even though it is made of cotton, and wind the *obi* around my middle; a Western dressing-gown is more sensible than a Japanese summer kimono, but most foreigners in Japan wear *yukata* in the same way that visitors to Kabul buy fur hats, tourists to Morocco buy *djellabahs*. One has a desire to identify oneself with the country one is living in.

"*Ohayo gozaimasu*," says Kazumi politely, when I have clambered down the stairs.

"Good morning." I see she has laid breakfast on the low dining table. "How good of you!"

She is dressed in a clean white sleeveless blouse and a blue cotton skirt. Her face has only the suggestion of make-up and her hair is done differently from last night; she has no fringe and her locks are pinned closely to her head. She looks the businesslike, efficient office girl she no doubt is. She fidgets with the knot in my *obi*, retying it; this is unnecessary as I shall have to undo the sash in the bathroom.

"I must go now. Kettle boiling, bread in toaster. I am sorry no corn flakes, no—"

"It doesn't matter. What time will you be back?"

She hesitates, then says, "Six or six-thirty."

"Goodbye till then."

"*Itte kimasu.*"

"*Itte irasshai.*"

She smiles at my Japanese reply, which means literally "going come back," places her feet into her shoes which are on the *genkan* step, opens the door very carefully, goes out, and slides the door to. I am pleased, for she is obviously not cross with me; after all, it is flattering to have an advance made to one.

I sit at the low dining table with my legs dangling into the pit below and push the lever on the toaster that lets fall the two slices of bread into the machine. As I am stirring the instant coffee the telephone rings. Watkins probably. The instrument is on the floor just behind me, two feet away; to lift the receiver I only have to stretch back my arm but I don't do so. I let the phone ring. I don't know why but I suddenly have a feeling that I do not want to see Watkins. I simply can't be bothered to behave conventionally and accept an invitation to dinner and then in a few days invite him back and so start a social round. The telephone stops ringing, but in a few seconds it starts again. As if to make excusable my ignoring of this persistent summons I struggle to my feet (really a table and chairs are much more practicable for eating than this "floor" nonsense!), pass into the sitting room, and pretend to myself that I am completely absorbed in a TV samurai film. It seems rather early in the morning for a tale of grisly violence (perhaps Japanese housewives like this sort of stuff), but better to see samurai grunting, losing their tempers, wielding their swords, and slashing one another, to hear blood-curdling yells and moans than to answer the telephone. I hate the telephone.

The daily maid arrives. She goes down on all fours and mutters words of respect and welcome. I like her at once. She reminds me of my Cambridge landlady, not by her act of obeisance, Mrs. Webb would never have done that, but by her face—gray hair, ruddy complexion, and very obvious false teeth. Her name is Misa-san; she has three grown-up children and she is motherly and plump.

How shall I delight Kazumi's palate this evening? Or is she one of those dull people who can't be wooed by good cooking?

I spend a happy morning consulting Curnowsky, the *Larousse*

Gastronomique, the *Gourmet Cookbook* (American), the *Esocoffier Cookbook*, and *Mastering the Art of French Cooking*. I consume many delicious dishes in my head. How about *daube de boeuf?* The book says it should be served with a *simple* red wine. I like "simple." Good French wine in Japan is expensive, and Japanese wine is far too costly for what it is: very *ordinaire*; but French *ordinaire* is within one's purse. The *daube* has to be marinated for three hours during which time it must be stirred frequently, and then it needs to simmer for four hours and still has to be stirred, *frequently*. Even for Kazumi (whom I desire) I won't spend seven hours in the hot kitchen. I am tempted to try Filet of Bison (Gamekeeper Manner). At the head of the recipe it says, under a drawing of a bucking bison, "Buffalo are no longer vanishing. . . ." I don't think I'd be able to purchase bison at a butcher's shop in Kyoto. I decide on a Curnowsky *menu d'été*: *Consommé froid en tasse* (I can buy a tin of clear soup and put it in the refrigerator); *Omelette au crabe* (canned crab is available everywhere); *Courgettes au beurre* (I shall miss this course): *Flamri à purée de framboise* (I shall substitute iced watermelon for this. It is much the same color).

To be a good cook one does not need to do the cooking. One has to have the ability to direct, that is all. So when Kazumi returns from her sedentary day in the office, I shall tell her exactly how to make an *omelette au crabe*.

I sleep most of the afternoon and have only written two lines of an article I am trying to do on Li Ho, the Chinese T'ang poet, when Kazumi returns.

"*Tadaima*," she cries. "I have come back."

"*Okaeri nasai*," I shout from my bedroom, where I am lying on my back under the fan.

I go below—the stairs force me to use a nautical term.

"Supper is ready except for a little cooking," I tell Kazumi.

She looks a bit wan and very hot; a strand of hair is stuck to her forehead, and there is a rivulet of sweat running down her neck; she is out of breath—has she been running? "You look hot. Why not have a short sit-down by the air conditioner before going into the kitchen?"

"I want to take a shower, may I?"

"Of course," I reply, badly concealing my irritation, for it is whiskey time and I want her to get some ice cubes out of the refrigerator. I hate freezing my fingers.

"Thank you." She smiles and leaves the room.

I get myself a large whiskey and on my way back from the kitchen I put two plates and some knives and forks on the dining table as a token effort. Not until my third whiskey does she emerge with her hair fuzzed up and her face more faded than it was last evening—is she going to be *complaisant* tonight?

"Look," I say, "I'm not sure where things are in the kitchen and it's hellish hot in there, so what I suggest is that I sit at the dining table and explain, or do you want a drink before eating?"

"No, thank you." Her dimpled smile is wistful. I think that this rather authoritative manner I've assumed may pay off.

"Right then. Let's move, shall we?" With a cry of, "God, what these Lafcadio Hearns will put up with!" I sink to the floor and sit at the wretchedly low table. From this position I can spy into the kitchen as the fusuma is open. "Now, Kazumi-san, if you open the refrigerator you will find a tin of *consommé* at the top. Please open the tin and bring it. I will serve it."

Kazumi does as I command. I should never dare to speak to my wife in this way; if I did, she'd simply say, "Do it yourself, duckie!" and I should. It's a mistake to marry a woman richer than oneself; money gives women an independence that is quite unsuited to their nature. In Japan things are more sensibly arranged: the wife obeys, or, at any rate, that is or was the theory.

When we have eaten our soup, Kazumi goes into the kitchen and half follows my instructions on how how to make a crab omelette; she thinks she knows how to do it, but she has too low a flame, she does not heat the pan first, nor does she keep the fork moving in the "Boulestin" manner. Why doesn't she know how to cook? With all these cookbooks in the house some occupant must have had some interest in the culinary art. The result of her ignorance is that I have to get up and give a demonstration in the middle of which the telephone rings.

"If it's for me, say I'm out," I tell Kazumi as she dashes to answer the intrusive call.

"It's Professor Watkins."

I wave my hand and shake my head. "No!" I say in a stage whisper.

Kazumi looks puzzled and then says, "Just a moment, please," and rejoins me at the stove, whose heat has made me break out in a gush of sweat. My shirt is wet through.

"It's Professor Watkins."

"So I heard. Why didn't you say I was out?"

"But you here!"

"Oh, all right!" I hand her the fork. "Keep it moving!" I squat by the telephone. "Peter Meadowes here . . . hello Bob! Marvelous to hear your voice! I arrived yesterday . . . did you? Maybe I didn't hear the phone . . . Yes, that was Kazumi-san. She's been showing me where things are and helping out. Bob, what about dinner the day after tomorrow? You and your wife, of course." Bob Watkins jumps at the invitation but says his wife cannot come. I imagine that he has adopted Japanese customs and rarely goes out with his wife. Sensible. I don't suppose she speaks much English and she would be a drag on the conversation.

The *omelette au crabe* turns out to be burnt scrambled egg mixed up with tough and stringy fiber—quite uneatable. We make do with bread and some cheese left over by my landlord; however, the watermelon is fairly filling; at least, after two large slices I don't want any more.

When Kazumi has done the washing up, I prevail upon her to stay a few days. She agrees, but I have a feeling that she does so because of the color television set and the air conditioner, not my powers of persuasion, nor my irresistibility, for she mentions that her set is a black-and-white one and her air conditioner is not working properly.

We look at TV again, but when I rise to go to bed, she makes not a glimmer of a suggestion to come with me in spite of my lingering look. Perhaps I should have been more insistent last night.

5

The electric bell in the girls' school on the other side of the main road, which my southern window faces, peals emphatically at eight a.m., like an alarm clock for the whole quarter, and awakens me from my second slumber—I wonder why it didn't wake me yesterday morning; perhaps my second slumber was deeper. My first slumber ended this morning at five-thirty, but I dropped off again after reading forty-two pages of *Justine* by D.A.F. De Sade, as the edition (no publisher's or printer's name given) calls the notorious yet maligned Marquis. The bookshelf in my bedroom shows eclectic tastes. Next to *Justine* is *The Conquest of Peru*; *Fanny Hill* has on one side *The Arts of Korea* and on the other Edith Sitwell's *Collected Poems*. If my reading lacks variety this summer, it will be my fault.

Kazumi has left before I get downstairs, therefore I am unable to ask her to do the shopping for tonight's dinner party in honor of Professor Robert T. Watkins, and Misa-san's duties are confined to cleaning and doing the laundry.

After I have read the *Japan Times* and the *Mainichi*, both of which contain almost identical news, I go upstairs, where Misa-san is passing the nozzle of the long trunk of the vacuum cleaner over the tatami. This doesn't do much good; it is a sort of ritual, a going through the motions. I tell her that she has done enough and obediently she detaches the pipe from the round dust container and struggles downstairs with the cumbersome contraption. She resembles my Cambridge landlady not only in her features (I noticed this morning that she also has the same brown eyes) but in her manner, too, for she has Mrs. Webb's cheeriness as well. When she doesn't understand my Japanese (the Kyoto dialect is different from that of Tokyo!), she roars with laughter and I can see Mrs. Webb laughing on my telling her that I had been gated for three weeks—"You'll 'ave to borrow me 'usband's 'at and coat then." And that laugh! It's so like Mrs. Webb's. It is a surprise to examine Misa-san's face and register that her nose is squat and her eyes are hooded, that she is Oriental; doing so is like being shaken out of a reverie; I am suddenly reminded that I am in Japan.

I spend a pleasant hour or so with my notebooks, fiddling physically with pieces of paper and pencils, and mentally with thoughts of

Kazumi, Noriko, my wife, my daughter, whom I hardly know, Mrs. Webb, Misa-san, and Li Ho, the Chinese T'ang poet about whom I am supposed to be writing.

The morning is periodically punctuated by the school bell followed by the buzz of girls' voices. I can see the tops of the girls' black heads in the classrooms, and their white blouses. When I have written "Li Ho was born in the seventh year of the reign of Emperor Te Tsang (A.D. 791) . . ." I decide it is time to go shopping for dinner tonight.

At six-thirty when I am sitting at my desk in the bedroom with a towel round my waist, the bell rings. Is it a punctual Bob or a late Kazumi who has forgotten her key? I expected the professor to arrive at seven and the woman to return at six. Slowly, I put on a shirt and a pair of slacks. It is Watkins.

"Hello, Bob! How delightful!"

"Well, the mystery man!" Watkins lowers his bulk on to the *genkan* step and takes off his shoes. His back is towards me and I have a view of the top of his pink scalp through his thin gray hair and of his bovine neck. He is sweating. With a grunt, he rises, turns, banging the chest of drawers and causing some of the water to spill out of the vase of gladioli.

"Come into the cool."

"Be glad to."

"Whiskey?"

"Please."

Watkins is a large man and when seated on one of the exiguous bench seats, the sitting room seems full. Perhaps he finds this land of the dainty and the minuscule attractive because he is so much the opposite of these qualities himself.

"Kazumi is staying here," I shout from the kitchen as I am preparing the drinks.

"Uh?"

"I'm expecting her back soon." I return to the sitting room and hand Watkins his whiskey. "Cheers!"

"Cheer-ho!" he replies, imitating my English accent and twinkling his blue eyes. "Scotch, eh? You say Kazumi-san is staying here?"

"Yes. I asked her to for a few days while I am settling in. Simpson apparently left her in charge as a caretaker."

"She usually acts as *rusuban* while he's away. One doesn't leave Japanese houses empty in case of fire and so on."

Bob is a little inclined to explain Japanese customs to everyone, but why to me? He must know that I am aware of this precaution. "Is Kazumi Oliver's mistress?" I ask.

"I've never been sure. It was Oliver's wife who took pity on Kazumi, and then when his wife died Kazumi helped him out a bit in the house. Oliver works out his paternal instinct on her perhaps. He has no children."

"Why didn't he adopt her?"

"I don't know. Oliver's wife, Betty, took Kazumi up when Kazumi's mother died. The mother worked in this house as a cleaning woman. She wasn't married, so Kazumi was a love-child or a lust-child." Bob laughed. "Then Betty died or was killed, rather, and Oliver kept up with Kazumi."

"How was Oliver's wife killed? Murder?"

"Nothing so dramatic. She was run over by a truck."

"Oh yes, I remember something about it now. Last year, wasn't it?"

"Last summer. She was crossing the street not far from here, that main street: Higashiyama-dori."

"How terrible!"

"In a way yes. They weren't getting on, you know."

"Because of Kazumi?"

"Maybe. I'm not sure."

"What's Kazumi do?"

"Some office job. Oliver and Betty sent her to a business school."

"Why hasn't she married?"

"Hard for her to find a Japanese husband with her background: illegitimate, her connection with foreigners. You know all the detective work that goes on before marriage. It would be impossible for her to conceal her past. She ought to marry, though; she must be getting on towards thirty."

Bob's words make me feel guilty about Noriko, but I can't marry her as I already have a wife and I told Noriko this from the beginning.

"I wonder where Kazumi is."

"You've fallen for her?"

"I haven't. It's simply that I'm expecting her back to dinner."

"Oliver told me that she had her wayward ways."

"You mean—?"

"She strayed sometimes. He never knew where she went."

"I wonder if she's straying tonight."

"Probably, but that shouldn't bother you, or—" Bob smiles, gives me a significant look—"Have you fallen for her?" He laughs, making the nostrils of his large nose dilate.

A door slides open and little bells tinkle. "Is that my door?" I ask anxiously.

"No, the one of the house opposite."

"Why the bell?"

"So the occupants are warned."

"I shouldn't want to be warned of an arrival at three in the morning, for example."

"You would if it were a burglar."

"Not even then, might have a knife."

"I can't for the life of me understand why you choose to come to Kyoto of all places for the summer. I'm pleased you did, mind, but you know well it's the hottest city in Japan at this time of the year."

"I came here to see you, Bob; and also, I've never been to your drama festival. No, seriously, I just happen to like Kyoto very much. Let's have another drink."

When the bottle is finished, we go out to a restaurant.

"What do you think happened to Kazumi?" I ask Bob for the umpteenth time.

"If you ask that question once more I shall know you are falling for her."

"What'll you have?"

"Dinner's on me," Bob insists.

"I invited you to dinner."

"You did all those drinks."

"Now, Bob . . ."

"I won't hear of it."

Bob is a nice chap.

One of the advantages of the shoe-taking-off business is that as soon as one opens the door one knows by the shoes in the *genkan* if someone has come back or not. Kazumi's gray suede shoes are not visible, but to make sure she is still out I climb the staircase to her bedroom. She is not there. I presume she is fed up with me and has gone to her apartment. This thought makes me want her even more.

The clappers from the temple opposite start up as soon as I get into bed. At first the clacks are slow and measured, then they break into waltz time, which seems improbable, but they do—a merry sutra? Now and again I hear the clip clop of *geta* passing down the lane. It's unlikely that Kazumi would go out in the clumsy wooden clogs used mostly by men, but all the same I listen anxiously when I hear the noise, which in its way is as haunting as the distant strumming of a samisen; and it is a summer noise. A bell rings. A caller for Kazumi? I turn on the light, but before I have got out of bed a door slides open and tinkling bells tell me that the late visitor is for the house opposite.

 I am reminded this morning that the wet season is not over, for the rain is pouring down in torrents, making such a roar that I feel I am excused from doing any writing. I spend the time in the bedroom looking at the water pelting onto the tiles of the outhouse and the temple roof, filling the gutters and flooding the garden. Misa-san asks me about Kazumi.

"She did not sleep here last night?" she asks.

"She slept in her apartment."

"*Aa so?* She slept in her *apato?* Is that so? *So?*"

"Yes. She told me she was going to sleep in her apartment last night." I must save face.

"*So?*"

"Yes."

An hour later after saying for the third time, "Isn't it coming down!" Misa-san repeats, "So Kazumi-san slept in her *apato* last night?" She is as curious as Mrs. Webb used to be about such matters.

"Yes."

"Is that so?"

"That is so."

Misa-san flicks a feather brush round the bedroom, where I am sitting, and goes slowly down the stairs. "What rain!" she says. She doesn't descend sideways as I do, but she clings tightly to the walls.

I try to go on with my essay on Li Ho, but only succeed in copying from my notebook the saying "To keep love fresh and passionate is as hard as trying to grow violets among nettles." How true! At least it is true as far as my affair with Noriko is concerned; the violets of love have all been stifled by the nettles of familiarity and staleness. My thoughts turn to Kazumi. Was she willing to act as caretaker out of the loyalty she feels she still owes Oliver? Or because she wanted to see what I was like and hoped to have an affair with me? If the last, why did she turn down my advances? Can it be that she doesn't find me attractive? Why did she not come home last night? I have no answers to these questions. All I know is that she has succeeded in worming herself into my mind, if not into my heart. I wonder if I had let my flat to someone like Simpson and put Noriko in charge, whether he would have had an affair with her. I fear not, for Noriko is not prone to stray; if she were, then my lust for her might not have waned.

The trouble with the rainy season is that it is also sticky hot and although a raincoat keeps the rain off, the sweat it generates causes one to get thoroughly damp from within. The answer is to have only an umbrella and not care about getting one's legs wet. Misa-san has only a flimsy, pink umbrella, a plastic affair, but at noon, when she has done her morning's work, she launches herself into the liquid lane with a smile, exclaiming, "It's still falling!"

I don't go out. What is the point of shopping for myself? If Kazumi is not going to be here, I shall not cook dinner for myself; to do so is miserable. I like to try out new recipes, but not on myself. I need a victim. I have bread and salami for lunch, then I read, sleep, read; after that I shower off the sweat in the bathroom and then I sit upstairs at the desk and scribble and moon, moon and scribble. I am encouraged in this almost non-activity by one of the Chinese philosophers I am studying who said, "Idle contemplation is superior to lively or clever action."

It is six o'clock, the rain has stopped, but there is no wind. I drip for half an hour, then go downstairs, find the evening newspaper stuck to the door, pour myself a whiskey, and repair to the coolness of the air-conditioned room.

After three whiskeys I feel tipsy, but this preprandial sensation is not exciting when one is alone and no dinner party is in the offing. I keep making arrangements about what to do when Kazumi returns. I look at my watch. "If she comes now," I say when it is seven-thirty, "I'll cook the steaks I bought for Bob last night."

At ten past eight I go out forlornly and walk all the way to Kawaramachi, the main street, and enter an air-conditioned steak restaurant. I sit at the counter on the other side of which are the chefs, properly hatted and aproned, the scullions, and the stoves. A couple at a table nearby stare and both of them smile when I order a steak and a whiskey in my bad Japanese. I wish the people of this country would get used to foreigners and stop regarding them as people from Mars. Japan or at least Tokyo and Kyoto have been infested with foreigners long enough for them to be accepted without curiosity. Are Japanese gazed at in London? I hope not. I am sure that if I lived here for thirty years I should still feel as conspicuous as I do not after five. Bob claims he is at home here, but Bob doesn't have much imagination.

My shirt is soaked with perspiration by the time I reach my lane. There is a pair of man's shoes on the *genkan* step and there is a light in the sitting room. Kazumi must be back. She is. I find her sprawled full length along one of the bench seats in a blue, sleeveless blouse and brief blue shorts to match; her legs and feet are bare and her head is propped up by an arm as she talks to a Japanese man with gapped teeth and thinning hair who is sitting on the other bench seat. She retains her languid pose when I enter, but he rises in the Western manner and seems embarrassed.

"Mr. Ohno," Kazumi says.

"How do you do!" Mr. Ohno and I chorus as we shake hands.

"Please," he says, waving a hand at his bench.

"No, no." I quickly sit on the floor.

Ohno seems uncomfortable. I feel as *de trop* as a cuckolded husband who has returned home a day earlier than expected.

Kazumi speaks to her friend in rapid Japanese, which I cannot follow. I wait for a pause and chip in with, "I waited for you last night. What happened?"

"Nothing. I spent in my *apato*." Kazumi then goes on with her Japanese conversation which I soon tire of listening to. I get up and slide open the fusuma.

"You going to bed?" she asks.

"Yes," I reply, curtly. "Good night."

Mr. Ohno rises.

"Good night," I repeat and leave the room.

"*Oyasumi nasai*," Kazumi cries after me in a cold singsong.

The first impulse that comes to me when I reach my bedroom is to go downstairs again and order Kazumi and her friend out of the house. I feel incensed at her rudeness: inviting a friend into what legally is my house; lolling on the sofa after my entrance; casually informing me that she has slept at her apartment. What right has she to behave in such a way: Does she think that she is aping Western manners? My sweat-heavy vest rips as I pull it over my head. "Damn her!" I exclaim as I hurl the garment into a far corner.

After some hesitation I decide that the way of dignity is not to go downstairs and order them out, but simply not to reappear, even though my staying upstairs means forgoing a shower and the cleaning of my teeth. My terse "good night" has shown my displeasure. The Japanese may be slow on the uptake when it comes to verbal subtleties in English, but they are very quick to sense a mood. Therefore I am certain that both Kazumi and her friend know that I, the master of the house, the *danna-san*, am annoyed, and despite her origin and subsequent westernization, respect for the master, the basic rule in Japanese society, is too deeply ingrained in her to have been completely eradicated.

I comfort myself with this thought and with de Sade's *Justine*. The former conjures up a scene of contrition in which Kazumi plays the main part, but the latter, though pornography usually leaves me cold, gives me prurient thoughts and makes me feel envious of what she and her friend may be getting up to in the sitting room. I don't imagine that the Japanese with the gapped teeth and the thinning hair is practicing any of de Sade's enormities, but nevertheless I am jealous.

My jealousy mounts as the torture perpetrated on Justine increases, so I get out of bed and begin to creep down the stairs; before I get to the bottom, the sitting room fusuma opens and I hear Kazumi see her friend off the premises.

He whispers, "*Oyasumi nasai.*" She replies, softly, "*Mata kite kudasai. Ki o tsukete kudasai.*" Then doors close and there are steps in the lane.

I go back to bed feeling relieved, and yet somewhat uncertain, for a lot can be accomplished in half an hour. And why should she say both "Please come again!" and "Please take care!"? I know these are conventional phrases, but was it necessary to use both of them?

7
I get up early, for during the period of wakefulness, which begins every morning at five-thirty, I decide that it would be clever tactics to be downstairs before Kazumi. I don't know exactly what I wish to say to her, but I am determined to be pretty scathing.

I put on an egg to boil and get hot and angry searching for an egg-cup, but none is to be found. I had forgotten that many Americans don't use egg-cups and peel their boiled eggs in a messy way and then eat them from a plate as if they were poached. Reminded that Queen Victoria's daughter experienced a similar lack of an egg-cup at the German Court, I copy the Prussian royal etiquette and use a liqueur glass.

I rehearse some imaginary scenes with Kazumi in which, in turn, I am hurt, then I am stern but reasonable like a father, then I am heavily sarcastic (the Japanese hate sarcasm), and finally I am a beast. In the last role I slap her twice across the face, first with the palm and then with the back of the hand and say, "Get out!"

While I am enacting in my mind the violent way of reproaching Kazumi, I hear her descend her staircase and go into the bathroom. Then, without any warning, she slides open the sitting room door and before I have been able to lower my newspaper she has murmured "Good morning" and gone into the kitchen. I go on looking at the paper; perhaps having been taken unawares I have hit on the best solution: I shall just ignore her. So when she passes through the sitting room again, I hide behind the newspaper and pay no heed to her second "Good morning."

I am still staring at the headlines when she returns and continue to do so, though I can see out of the corner of my eye that she is standing over me. Obstinately, childishly, I refuse to recognize her presence. Then, suddenly, she bends over the top of my frail barricade and plants a kiss on my head. "I come back six-thirty," she says and is out of the room, into her shoes, and down the lane before I have collected my wits, which her startling action has scattered in all directions.

The spot which her lips lightly touched tingles as from a blessing or an accolade and I sit stunned for a while, only giving Misa-san a vague nod on her entrance. I remain in a daze most of the morning, sitting with my back to the desk looking out of the window at the temple wall and thinking of Kazumi, who, of course, is forgiven. After I have grunted farewell to the bowing maid, I take some of the cookery books down from their shelf with the object of deciding about dinner. What shall I give her? I settle on goulash after an unsatisfactory perusal of the books whose recipes seem too complicated for the simple shopping I can do in the vicinity. Goulash is easy; it is one of my specialties.

I am so hot after cutting up onions and chopping meat in the kitchen that I spend the afternoon in the air-conditioned room and do not go upstairs until five o'clock. On the way I notice on the floor of the *genkan* an air-letter from my wife. I do not even bother to pick it up and continue up the stairs to the bedroom, where I resume my study of the temple roof and the fig tree among whose dark green leaves, I now notice, little round buttons are burgeoning. There is a gray tradesman's van in the temple compound and a woman is taking down the drenched washing outside the subsidiary temple building, which, I think, must be let off as apartments. How dare my wife write to me! I suppose she got my Kyoto address from my bank. It was quite wrong of the manager to divulge my whereabouts. Her letter is an intrusion. I wanted to spend the months of July and August cut off from her and from any thoughts of her, and now she is pushing herself into my life, and during the summer holidays too. I decide not to read the letter; after five minutes, though, I go downstairs and fetch it. It bears a London postmark. Well, she often goes to London.

God! My wife says she is planning to come out here next month. She has been invited to stay with some friends (the Crawfords; I know them) in San Francisco and thinks of coming on to Japan. She has arranged for our daughter to be with some cousins. I don't want Monica here. I shall write and tell her that the humid heat is worse than ever this summer, is quite unbearable in fact, and suggest that she either cancel her visit or postpone it until the autumn. She proposes, quite unpractically, that I should return to England with her. "Resign from your silly job," she says. She doesn't realize, never did, that one has certain obligations and that a contract is a contract; because of her money, she has been spoiled all her life and has always been able to get out of any commitments she hasn't wished to fulfill, and she imagines that anyone can do the same.

If she really is coming out, I must hurry up and make hay while the sun shines.

By six-thirty the goulash is ready and I have mashed the potatoes, laid the table, drunk one whiskey, and read the evening paper, but Kazumi does not return until after seven, by which hour the goulash is still ready and the potatoes have begun to burn and I have had three whiskeys.

"*Tadaima!*" she cries.

"*Okaeri nasai,*" I reply, stirring the stew.

Kazumi comes into the kitchen. "I am sorry."

"You did say six-thirty." I can't help being prickly.

"They kept me at the office."

"The potatoes are beginning to burn."

"I'm sorry."

She looks sorry too, sorry and concerned; she looks hot. Generously, I suggest she has a shower and gratefully she accepts the offer; therefore by the time she comes to the table in her very brief shorts, sleeveless blouse, and no stockings, I am feeling rather smug. In spite of her protestations I insist on her sitting at the table and my serving the goulash, and to make her feel even more under an obligation I pointedly give her the larger helping and put some of the burnt mashed potato on my plate. As soon as I have made the effort of getting down on the floor and putting my legs under the table, I notice that I have forgotten the salt, so martyrlike, I start to rise. At once she rises, and being younger and nimbler than I she is on her feet first.

"What do you want?"

"The salt."

"I get."

"No." I am standing now and near the kitchen door. "I'll get it."

"Please."

"I insist."

When I have returned from the kitchen, she is sitting down again, but she has changed the plates round.

With a grunt I drop to the floor. "Why did you do that?" I hand back her plate.

"No. I like this one."

"No," I say severely, "that one is mine."

"No." She is firm. "*Itadakimasu.*" She begins to eat. "Very delicious," she says before she has had time to taste it properly.

"Too liquid," I say, deprecatingly.

"Very delicious. *Oishii.*"

Her praise, which I enjoy, is interrupted by a siren and a bell.

"Fire!" she cries. "Fire!" She leaps up as if under a hypnotic compulsion and dashes out of the house. I follow, but not until I have had my fill of goulash. The Japanese don't care if their food is hot or cold. I do. Down the lane housewives, husbands, grandfathers, children, grandmothers are running, not away from the fire, to safety, but towards it, to watch. There is not much to see: only black smoke billowing out of the first floor window of a shop in the nearby main street. The fire engines have arrived and numerous firemen in blue uniforms and black lacquer helmets are milling around getting out hoses, moving furniture from the stricken room. I return to the goulash with Kazumi.

"Who was he?" I ask, knowing that Kazumi will realize that I am referring to her visitor of last night.

Without surprise, she says, "A friend."

"Lover?"

"Just a friend," she replies, putting some cold stew into her mouth. "Very delicious, really. Very delicious."

"It's easy to make. Tell me about your friend."

"I've known him long time. He's married. Sometimes he visit me. I did not know he was coming. He came to the house soon after I come home."

"Does Oliver know him?"

"Yes, of course. Oliver-san he like him very much."

"I see." But I don't really understand at all. Oliver Simpson seems odder than ever: he allows his ward or his mistress to act as his caretaker and has been, for some time apparently, compliant about her having friends like Mr. Ohno. Perhaps Oliver likes three-somes. He becomes more puzzling each day and I wish I had met him.

I do not protest when Kazumi offers to do the washing up, nor do I help her. It is, after all, more of a woman's task than cooking. Also, I know sufficient about Japanese psychology to realize that it is a mistake to put anyone too much under an obligation. Her washing the dishes will in her simple mind balance my having done the cooking, and we shall be equal, but to be completely equal in my mind I must return the morning kiss.

Impatiently, I wait for her to join me in the sitting room. I sit on the floor with my back against the bench seat, hoping that she'll sit beside me when she has finished. The washing-up noises cease and Kazumi enters the room.

I pat the tatami. "Come and sit down."

"*Terebi?*"

"All right."

She switches on the set, goes back to the kitchen, and in a few moments reappears with an iron and a legless ironing board which she places on the floor. The iron is plugged in and stood on its end. Then she fetches a pile of blouses and underwear and proceeds to iron these garments sitting on her heels and now and then glancing at a guess-the-tune game. I realize that doing such prosaic tasks after dinner in the sitting room is quite normal and not meant to be insulting (so many Japanese houses or flats have one room for sleeping, eating, sitting, and ironing), nonetheless I find it irritating. I get up.

"Going out?" she asks, not looking up from the ironing board.

"A walk."

"*Itte irasshai,*" she says, making the first fold in a blouse.

8 I wander down the road past the shop that has just had the fire. About thirty firemen are sitting on benches outside in the road (there is no pavement) and merrily drinking sake. The shopkeeper is fussing over the guzzling firemen, opening bottles, passing apples; he wears the worried expression of a man who is host to superior and demanding guests that he is obliged to entertain. Written on the faces of the firemen are the marks of self-satisfaction and self-importance that victory brings. Custom no doubt demands that the owner of the "saved" premises should reward the firemen; he must rid himself of his immediate obligation to them in the same way that Kazumi relieves herself of her burden of obligation to me by washing the dishes.

A few years ago when my wife was in England and my affair with Noriko was at its height, I returned home two hours later than promised to find Noriko coming down the stairs from my apartment to which she had the key.

"Why you late?" she asked, her face cross and tearful.

"The party went on longer than I thought it would."

"You said it was only a cocktail party and you'd be back at eight-thirty."

"Oh God, does it matter all that much?"

"Yes, does it matter." She ran down the stairs and out.

I did not follow her. I let myself into the apartment and began to pack—I was going on a tour of Kyushu the following day. Although it was not a Saturday, Noriko was to have spent the night with me as it was my "last night" in Tokyo for three weeks. I found a note from her on my desk. "I go out alone sad. I am very foolish. What can I do? I don't know what can I do."

The veiled threat this note seemed to contain unsettled me, partly for selfish reasons, as I did not want a scandal: "Married Englishman's Japanese girlfriend throws herself under train . . ." The press would certainly rub in the fact that I was married and suggest that I was having a passing affair with Noriko. Fear that one's mistress may run out and commit suicide is constantly at the back of the mind of any Westerner who has an affair with a Japanese, for to a Japanese who has lost face (and loss of face can occur without the foreigner realizing it), lost hope, been seriously frustrated, the world may suddenly become all black and the only apparent solution is to put an end to oneself. I was worried, therefore, when I read the note and angry with Noriko for making me worried, for spoiling my holiday on the eve of my departure. Noriko had possibly further lost face by meeting me unexpectedly on the stairs; she had obviously expected to get away before I returned. Was Noriko capable of throwing herself under a train? A common method of suicide in Japan. I was beginning to think she had done so and to wonder what I should do. I would have to see her parents (a thing I have always avoided doing), go to the funeral—the whole experience would be ghastly and sad. Just as I had buried Noriko and tried to console her parents with a large check there was the sound of a key being inserted in the lock. Her face was streaked with tears and she flung herself at once into my not very welcoming arms.

"When I go out," she sobbed, "I think I never see you again, but as I walk to the station I remember that everything I wear came from you: my ring, my watch, the stuff for this coat, this dress you bring from Hong Kong. . . ." As she clasped me my eyes caught her cheap little handbag, which she was clutching, and I made a mental note to buy her a handbag next.

The apparent reason for forgiving my "monstrous" behavior (I really think that whenever I was somewhere for longer than I said I would be she believed I was in bed with someone) was because she felt under an obligation. The immediate mention of my practical presents shows this. According to her reckoning her obligation to me at that moment was greater than mine to her (I had incurred an obligation to her by taking her on as a mistress), and it was the feeling of obligation that brought her scurrying back as much as that of affection. The incident marked the beginning of the decline in my affair with Noriko.

After sauntering round the streets, my shirt is soaked and my trousers cleave uncomfortably to my legs, but I am purged of the feeling of exasperation which overcame me while watching Kazumi iron her clothes. The district has enchanted me and I enter the house with the same feeling of elation one has from seeing a perfect piece of art or hearing a consummate rendering of a concerto.

The sitting room light and the television are still on, so I know that Kazumi has not gone to bed. I slide open the door and there she is in her brief shorts and sleeveless blouse, lying full length on the bench seat in the same position she was in last night, but now she is alone, or more or less alone, for she is watching television and the box engrosses her as much as Mr. Ohno.

She does not get up or go down on all fours and touch the tatami with her forehead as used to be the custom when the master of the house came home, she just flicks her eyes at me and says, "Where did you go?" Before I have replied she is again looking at the screen.

"Just for a walk. I think I'll have a shower."

I have a mad idea that if I am also in the state of seminudity an approach may be easier. After the shower I sit on the other bench seat with a towel round my waist trying hard to hold in my belly. "Is this a good play?" I ask, referring to the domestic drama on the screen that for the last ten minutes has consisted of a conversation among a lower middle class family who are sitting on the floor of their living room.

"Yes," Kazumi replies, not turning her head. She has the TV look on her face, the vacant gape television addicts acquire.

I wait for the commercials to interrupt her absorption, but they don't; they seem as compelling to her as the play, and they can't be, for even I, a reluctant and intermittent viewer, have seen them dozens of times. The only excuse I can find for her is that she is so deeply under the TV spell that she is physically incapable of breaking it. I make this excuse for her, because to admit to myself that she is purposely ignoring my advances would hurt my vanity.

The wretched drama begins again.

I slip off the bench onto the floor, brushing my hand against the arm that is supporting her head. She moves her arm slightly.

The drama continues. The family are still on the floor of the same room, but now they are eating at a table similar to the one in my dining recess, and their legs are tucked under them, not dangling into a hole.

Suddenly, I get up and stand between her and the screen, bend over, and kiss her on the mouth. She responds, but with her teeth clenched, and then sticks out an arm for me to move aside.

"Excuse me," she says.

"I am going to bed."

"*Oyasumi nasai*," she replies, her eyes on the screen.

 The telephone bell makes such a tiny tinkle that when I'm upstairs I can only hear it if I'm not typing or if there's a lull in the traffic; and even if I do hear it I can pretend I haven't with a clear conscience. But this morning Misa-san, who always hears it, answers the ring. Noriko has telephoned to say she has got leave from her company and will be coming down for three nights at the end of the month.

"Is she still with you?"

"Yes."

"Why?"

I stumble. "Well, er, er, I find her useful."

"What do you mean?" Noriko is more outspoken on the telephone than she is to my face.

"I don't like sleeping in this house alone and she knows where everything is. . . ."

Very sarcastically, in a tone of voice she has learned from me, Noriko replies, "I see." I can visualize her twitching her little, *retroussé* nose in disapproval.

"There is nothing for you to be jealous about."

"I am not jealous."

Neither of us speak for an agonizing twenty seconds. Finally, I say, "See you on the thirty-first then. Let me know the time of your train. I'll meet you at the station."

"Thank you," she says meekly.

"Not at all."

"See you later." I have stopped her saying "See you again," an expression I detest and one which is overused and misused in Japan.

"All right then." For some reason I am loath to ring off as I don't want to upset her.

At last she says goodbye and I am free from her. But am I? The extraordinary thing is that Noriko has a hold over me; her goodness, her devotion, her constancy make me feel guilty. I feel much more of a swine when I have been unfaithful to Noriko than I do after I have deceived my wife. Perhaps the reason is that my wife is English with the same kind of background and education as I, and is capable of not only standing up for herself but of giving me a thorough dressing down; she is taller than I too, and this advantage no doubt gives her a feeling of superiority; whereas poor Noriko can't express herself properly in my tongue and I can only half understand what she says in hers; also, her head only comes up to my chin.

It is hard to believe that four years ago I spent most of the day thinking about Noriko and whenever the telephone rang I dashed to it expectant and thrilled, my heart thumping. This falling out of love is as inexplicable as falling in love; one no more wants, in the sense of having a conscious desire, to fall in love than one wills an affair to end—something happens, something snaps that is beyond control. Today it seems incredible that I once thought Noriko to be the most wonderful person on earth, that I used to get worked up on Saturdays when I often took her to Kabuki. I put it down to the fact that I was new to Japan and that anything Japanese fascinated me, above all Japanese girls.

The difference between my gangling, tweed-skirted, jersey-with-pearls wife and a delicate, small-featured, petite Japanese girl seemed as great as the difference between two species. My wife had never been attractive, nor had she ever been very feminine; the only kind epithet one could in all honesty apply to her was "handsome." When we married in 1958 she was thirty-seven and I was twenty-eight. Why did we get married? We got on well, we made each other laugh, we both wanted to travel, and we both had enough money for me not to worry about having a serious career—we were both only children and each of us had inherited tidy sums from our respective parents (to my eternal annoyance my wife's inheritance was the larger). I met her in London when I was on leave from a teaching post in Beirut. We were married in three weeks. She was very keen to go to Lebanon. I think in a way she regarded herself as a latter-day Lady Hester Stanhope. When we got to Lebanon, which had just recovered from internal upheavals, we rented a large, rambling, Turkish-style house with marble floors and a roof of pink tiles in a coastal village north of the capital. Monica took a great interest in the house, making alterations, buying endless Arab, Persian, and Turkish antiques, and reviving the garden which had fallen into decay. Our existence in Lebanon was not all honey and wine, but it was pleasant enough and we spent six years there. What made it agreeable was the four-month-long summer holiday during which we made lengthy motor journeys; one year we traveled all over Persia and Turkey, another we motored along the North African coast to Tangier, and once across Iran to Kabul; three times we drove across Turkey and the Balkans to England. Monica was at her best on these trips; she was an excellent driver and didn't mind rough accommodations or coarse food; our journeys passed in harmony; we both had an interest in Moslem and Byzantine architecture and happily we would drive miles out of the way over bumpy roads to see a ruin.

And then one May our daughter was born. At forty-two Monica had a difficult time over the birth and was unable to travel that summer and I, selfishly, went off alone on a tour of the Far East. Japan went to my head like a double dry martini taken before breakfast. I was enchanted. Everyone seemed considerate, sweet, engaging, and no one cared much about politics, a subject which the Arabs cannot leave alone; it was refreshing to find people interested in other things. Three days before I was due to leave I met Noriko on a train (she was returning to Tokyo from her parents' home in Shimane-ken, a prefecture on the Japan Sea coast) and I stayed.

Monica was puzzled at first, then annoyed. I managed to get a post at one of the many universities in Tokyo and I have been there, on and off, ever since. Monica came out twice, but she didn't like

Japan. I think the main reason was the men, whom she found puny and unattractive; this was subconscious, I am sure, for Monica has never been much interested in sex. But I know she approved of Arab men, admiring their rugged looks, their masculine ways. She hated populous Tokyo and city life in a flat and having to struggle with another foreign language (she had made great strides in Arabic); Monica liked the wild hills of Lebanon, the desert wastes of Syria and Jordan, the gallant, expansive gestures of the Arabs, the spontaneous generosity of the poor. She loathed the lush Japanese countryside with its neat valleys of rice paddies and thickly wooded hills as much as the constant crowds, the sprawling urbanization; the frequent giggles she evoked because of her height infuriated her. The longest she stayed in Japan at any one time was three months, and when she was here it was a period of strain (partly because of Noriko, whose existence I successfully concealed from her) and it was a relief for both of us when she left with the child. It was as if Japan was on trial in our apartment, for most of the time we would argue about the country: she attacking, I defending.

Because of the disturbed state of the Middle East, Monica went to live in the spacious country house in Suffolk which we had bought one summer and left in charge of a gardener and his wife. There she was able to organize the garden, redecorate the house, and look after our daughter. Now the girl is at boarding school, the house and the garden have had everything done to them that could be done and Monica is getting restless and bored—that is why she is going to stay with the Crawfords in San Francisco next month and come on here afterwards. I noticed that she was unsettled last summer when I spent two months in England. I did not suggest that she return to Japan with me, nor did she. I agreed, though, that I would spend one final year in Japan and then come home to stay. We did not have more than one or two discordant days and we seemed to recapture some of the delight we had found in each other's company before and just after our marriage; another reason for the unusual lack of tension was that there had always been at least one friend staying with us and we paid frequent visits to London. I enjoyed the rather hectic social time we had during those two months because, although I'm not very keen on such activity, it was such a change from the dreary parties one finds oneself going to in Japan, parties at which the Japanese guests and the foreign guests divide into ethnic groups. I was no longer in love with Noriko; in fact by the end of August when I was due to return I had fallen out of love with Japan and almost in love with England (the glorious summer weather had something to do with my attitude, I'm sure—summer in Japan is horridly hot); in addition, Monica was fifty-seven and was beginning, I sensed, to feel the effect of having married someone younger than herself and to fear the possibility of a lonely old age. I think that was the reason for her never mentioning divorce, perhaps considering it better to be married to a truant husband than not to have one at all.

It is strange this love-hate emotion I have had for Monica and for Japan. My feelings towards Japan have corresponded with my feelings towards Noriko, and my feelings toward Monica have changed with my feelings towards the West. Now, in Kyoto, in this steaming rice bowl, as the Japanese call their ancient capital in the summer, my affection for Japan has revived, and Kazumi, I suppose, is responsible.

At midday after Misa-san has gone I go out to the shops. The sky is overcast and the humidity and the temperature are high. I call at the usual shops whose owners and assistants are beginning to know me and to be friendly. There is a greengrocer's I enjoy going to because the old man in charge is so courteous, always giving me a deep bow and saying "excuse me" when I hand over the money for my purchase as if taking it from me is unfair extortion. His wife will never let me have the apples that are on display and insists on opening a fresh box. Shopping at the local shops is a pleasure even in the overpowering heat, and I understand why the housewives do it twice a day.

It comes on to rain while I am struggling home loaded with brown paper parcels. A girl runs out of one of the shops I don't often patronize with an umbrella which has the name of the shop written on each panel; as my arms are full, she puts the umbrella over my head and fits the handle under one of my fingers.

This spontaneous gesture of kindness makes my day (I take it as such and not as a calculated one to entice my custom) and I spend the rest of it in a good mood, in spite of the fact that I have to stoop over the hot stove for hours making Bolognese sauce. I am giving Kazumi spaghetti Bolognese tonight.

Kazumi returns from work soon after six, so she is able to cook the spaghetti and warm up the sauce. She says politely, "*Itadakimasu*" (which means "I shall eat now" and is the equivalent of saying grace or *bon appetit*), before starting to eat, and "*Oishii*" ("delicious") three times while she is eating. I don't mind the way she lowers her head and sucks the spaghetti noisily into her mouth; however, I should discourage Noriko from eating in this off-putting way. At the end Kazumi puts her hands together and mutters, "*Gochisosama*," which is a formal expression used automatically after every meal however good or bad. It translates as "it has been a feast," but since it is used too much and indiscriminately it means no more than "thank you."

I find Kazumi's "undress" house costume of tiny shorts and flimsy blouse most provoking, and while she stands at the sink washing the dishes, I cannot keep my eyes off her bare, glabrous legs, her neat, round buttocks, and the back of her slender neck—her hair is piled on top of her head tonight, a style that suits her. With an effort I keep my hands off and we sit watching television like a married couple tired of each other's bodies. Her favorite program of the week is on. This is a song and dance show introduced by a famous actor called Saburo Yamamura, and known affectionately by maidens, wives, and matrons as Sabu-chan. Saburo is twenty-three and handsome. He is stalwart and manly; he has thickish eyebrows that tilt upwards, clear-cut features, and a devastating smile; his hair covers his ears but it is tidy and some strands are allowed to fall over his forehead in a careful-careless fashion. He wears a white sweater with the sleeves rolled up his shapely arms as far as his elbows, black flared trousers, and black boots with pointed toes. He sings inexpertly, or rather in a deep voice murmurs absurdities about lost love into a microphone while pretending to play a guitar, and he dances amateurishly in front of a chorus of skinny damsels and girlish boys. Kazumi adores him. When I point out his deficiencies as a singer and a dancer, she becomes indignant.

"I don't care," she says. "I like him. He is a very good actor."

"He can't sing."

"He sings very well."

"He can't dance."

"He is very charming."

I am quite jealous of Saburo, envious of his age and his looks, and I think Kazumi senses this and praises him highly on purpose to tease me. I leave her enveloped in admiration and desire (?) for her idol and go upstairs to work on my Chinese philosophers. I am pleased to record this remark of Li Ho's: "If love is something permanent or a thing that is forever assured, it is no longer a human relationship but a social habit."

The fact that I don't know if Kazumi likes me or not gives edge to my existence. But if she doesn't like me, why does she stay? Is it only the air conditioner and the color television set that keep her here? Why, if she is indifferent, did she thank me so politely for the spaghetti Bolognese? Was it just automatic thanks? Why if she has no feelings towards me, did she give me that kiss? When I have asked myself these questions I realize that I am falling in love, or, to be honest, have begun seriously to lust after her.

10 Love or lust has a curious effect; either one or the other made me get up early this morning and prepare breakfast, which Kazumi and I have together on the floor at the dining table for the first time since my arrival. Usually I eat my corn flakes, boiled eggs, and toast in the sitting room and Kazumi bolts down whatever she has in the kitchen as she's in a hurry. She thanks me several times for this attention, and when she gets to her feet, I rise too and see her off at the front door, gazing after her until she has turned onto the main road at the bottom of the lane. If she weren't used to the idiosyncrasies of foreigners, she would be quite bemused by my behavior: a Japanese man would not behave like a housewife however infatuated he was.

In spite of the intermittent rain and the intense heat I pass the day in a rapture thinking of Kazumi. At noon I walk to the center of the city, a distance of over a mile, and although I am drenched with sweat I feel exultant. Everything delights me: the rushing canal, the trickling river, the lowering clouds hanging over the dark green hills, the girls in the supermarket where I shop extravagantly, helping myself to a pineapple from the Philippines, Gruyère, French wine, and asking the butcher to cut me two fillet steaks.

I want to buy Kazumi a present but I don't know what to get. I wander down the main street looking in shop windows, my parcels getting heavier and more awkward. Finally, in a department store, I decide on a bamboo brooch that is quite pretty, the bamboo being shredded as thin as wire and tied in a bow to look, at least, at first glance, a bit like spun gold.

"Tonight Yoiyama," Kazumi says as soon as she has come into the kitchen, where I am sweating over the steaks.

"What's that?"

"The night before Gion Festival. Everyone goes out."

"Oh," I say, betraying disappointment. I had pictured a leisurely dinner ending with my presenting the bamboo brooch.

"Don't you want to go out?"

"Yes, of course." I had forgotten about the festival; there was nothing to remind me of it in the main street this morning. So instead of a slow, civilized meal we have a rushed one. Kazumi leaves half her expensive steak, has only a sip of wine, declines the cheese, and gobbles several slices of the pineapple, which I have soaked in Cointreau (my landlord's). I might just as well have given her sandwiches. The Sauce Bearnaise over which I labored for an hour means nothing to her—it could have been jam, and if the wine were corked she wouldn't notice. I took the trouble to see that the potatoes and the steak were hot, but it wouldn't have mattered if I had cooked them in the morning, put them in the refrigerator, and served them iced. I am saddened more than annoyed. Of course she used those empty words of praise *oishii* and *gochisosama*. I should have known better, for Noriko is much the same and has never really liked Western food. Her two favorite dishes are salad and scrambled eggs. The trouble is that one always hopes that one's latest love will be perfect.

I don't know if Kazumi wants me to go with her to join the

crowds examining the shrine cars that she has explained are parked outside the houses of the protagonists in tomorrow's procession, or whether she wants to be with her Japanese friends (the man with the gapped teeth and the thinning hair, for example), so when she has changed into a pretty blue dress, put on pearl earrings and a pearl necklace (which reminds me of Monica, whose neck must be twice the size of Kazumi's), and is ready to leave, I hesitate.

"You do not want to see the people? Everyone goes out tonight."

"May I come with you?"

She looks surprised. "Of course."

"I'll just go and change my shirt."

"That one all right."

"I won't be a minute."

My object in going upstairs is to get the bamboo brooch and give it to her; her willingness for me to accompany her has wiped away my feelings of irritation over the meal and I want to reward her. I change my shirt and before going downstairs I unwrap the brooch to see if it will do. It looks cheap (which it was) and will obviously not go with pearls. Why didn't I buy a pearl one? I curse my meanness and put the brooch in a drawer. I shall give it to Noriko and buy Kazumi a pearl one.

11 When I am walking in the street with Noriko I often feel that we are being regarded with disapproval. I am sure that I am right in interpreting some of the glances she receives as meaning, "Why are you with a foreigner?" and some of the ones I get as, "Why should you have one of our women?" Such patriotism or xenophobia is natural I suppose—would I be pleased if my daughter wanted to marry a black? Nevertheless, it is disconcerting for the foreigner. I have spoken about this to Noriko and she agrees that sometimes the looks are hostile; however, one grows accustomed to anything and when I am with Noriko I try and fend off a glare with a smile.

There is nothing that can be done about this problem for it

would be impossible for me to become a Japanese; even if I were nat-uralized, I should not be Japanese; I could never look Japanese, never speak or write Japanese perfectly, never be accepted as a Jap-anese. And how ridiculous I would feel when I told people, old Eng-lish friends for example, that my nationality was Japanese! Noriko has acquired some of my mannerisms and they don't wear well on her. She raises her eyebrows and gestures more than ordinary Japa-nese girls do; she takes longer strides, she says "jolly good!" "right-ho!" and "really" and these exclamations sound silly on her lips.

Another thing that makes me feel shy about being with Noriko is her age. At twenty-five (she was a university student when I first met her) she is twenty-three years younger than I and I certainly don't look less than my age with that railway junction on my fore-head, those shipping lines which lead out from the corners of my eyes when I smile, that bulge at my belt, my brindled hair, which now resembles the coat of a Cairn terrier. If Noriko were European, she could pass as a daughter or a niece, but since she is Japanese our relationship is obvious; pretending she is my secretary is rather a farce. I am probably too self-conscious, for very few people can pos-sibly care about us, and my embarrassment emanates from a feeling of guilt. Consciously, I don't mind being an adulterer and a fornica-tor; subconsciously, I suppose I do. I don't think Noriko has any feel-ing of sin about our relationship, even though I am married—to have a mistress is almost respectable in Japan. She would consider it wrong, though, if I were unfaithful to her, not wrong in a moral sense, but wrong because we are supposed to be lovers. I have, in fact, and once she found out about my infidelity.

My affair with Noriko had been going for about two years and I was beginning to get tired of her. I didn't want to tire of her; I just did. One night after a party I went to a bar and brought home a hostess for the night, and foolishly both she and I overslept and the daily maid, a gossiping widow, arrived before we were up. Madden-ingly, the hostess, whom I had found to be a very bad value for the £40 I had to pay her, had a chat with the maid while I was in the bathroom.

The following Sunday I went out to buy some nuts and rice bis-cuits to have with the drinks at the lunch party I was giving at noon while Noriko helped the maid prepare the meal. Noriko would sometimes make herself useful in this way and she did so with considerable tact, setting in front of guests, who might disapprove of our connection, as if she were an extra maid hired for the occasion. She enjoyed doing this because it meant staying with me longer than I usually allowed her to and also because she was amused by the "game" we played of giving each other surreptitious love signals such as touching hands while she served me, winking (she could only blink actually), or even stealing a quick kiss when the guests were not looking—she derived pleasure from the fact that she knew me better, or, at least, more intimately, than did my friends. While I was mixing some more dry martinis in the dining room before lunch on that Sunday morning, I suddenly whispered to Noriko, who was by my side with a tray, "I love you."

"Is it true?" she asked earnestly.

"Of course."

"Really?"

"Yes."

"Say it again."

"What?"

"Say you love me."

"Why?"

"Please."

"All right, I love you." But I said it without conviction the second time. I don't know why I had uttered the words in the first place, possibly because she had been working hard on my behalf and I had drunk three dry martinis. The meal passed off smoothly, but I got no return wink or blink from Noriko, nor did she allow her hand to touch mine while she was serving me.

After lunch I had arranged to go with two of my guests to watch an amateur Sumo tournament and as I was getting into their car, Noriko said, "Who is Akiko?"

I had truly forgotten that that was the name of the wretched hostess.

"Who?"

"Akiko."

"I don't know whom you mean." Blushing, I wrenched my coat free from her grasp and got into the car.

But she held the door. "Please answer my question." Her little brown eyes were watering and her expression was desperate. "Is it true?" she demanded.

"What?" I asked, irritably. Her behavior was becoming acutely embarrassing, for Mr. and Mrs. Geddes were already seated in the front of the car.

"Is it true?" she repeated determinedly between her teeth.

"No," I lied. "Of course it isn't."

"Really?" Oh that "really," with almost my intonation! How it used to madden me and more so than ever at that moment!

"Yes." I pushed her hand away and she slammed the door and we drove off.

"What was that all about?" inquired Mrs. Geddes, intrusively.

"I don't quite know. Some disagreement in the kitchen, I think. She and the cook don't get on, I fancy."

"I expect she's in love with you," said Mrs. Geddes.

"Not possible." I forced a laugh.

"You never know with these people. They try to hide a secret passion and then all of a sudden it pops out."

"Really?"

The next day, although it was a Monday, Noriko came to see me and for the second time I feared she was going to kill herself. I admitted the whole truth about Akiko, explaining that she had only slept in the apartment once and that I did not intend to see her again, that it was only a passing dalliance performed when I was drunk. We went for a walk and sat on a bench in a park by the railway. I was contrite which, I now realize, was foolish because it was weak. Women, at least Japanese women (not Monica), respect strength. I reiterated abject apologies for about an hour while she cried; her crying unnerved me for she did it openly, not seeming to mind that passers-by were noticing me with distaste. When we parted on that Monday afternoon I was exceedingly worried for she had left me with a frog in her throat and her face streaked with tears. I returned to the apartment and took out a little of the anger I felt on the maid, whom I severely reprimanded for gossiping about my private affairs. I nearly sacked her, but she was a good cook so I didn't.

For the next few weeks Noriko behaved as if she had been told that she had cancer or had suffered some terrible family tragedy. She would be pleasant and smiling for a while but in a way that suggested that she was being brave, then she would break down. If only I had been strong enough and not allowed her to extract from me such heavy payment for my lapse, which in any case had given me no pleasure. For some reason, because I feel responsible, perhaps, Noriko has a hold over me which seems stronger than the bond of marriage. One cannot divorce a mistress and so it can be that a mistress is more difficult to get rid of than a wife. I suppose I could buy her off, but the very idea seems sordid and distasteful. I would not have the courage to broach the subject.

12 Kazumi and I take a taxi towards the center of the city, but because of the crowds we have to get out before we have gone very far. The main streets are packed with human beings pressed as tightly together as in a commuter train; it is only just possible to stand, and it is hot, very hot—one is relieved on such occasions that the Japanese are an exceedingly clean people with a mania for bathing.

We edge ourselves very slowly down Shijo Street, where, at intervals, are parked the huge shrine cars that are pulled by men in loincloths and short cotton coats in the festival procession. The upper part of each wagon is filled with youths in blue and white *yukata* with white bands round their heads and in their hands they hold the heavy copper cymbals, which are clanged in a slow, plangent rhythm, or flutes, which are made to emit a weird whine. We push on. I am in favor of retiring to a bar in a side street, but Kazumi wants to see every single float. Going with the stream of the multitude we shuffle across a main street into a residential quarter where the smaller floats, like large palanquins, are on view outside various houses. Some of the houses have their family treasures on show as is the custom on this evening, and Kazumi wants to look at all the screens and kimonos displayed in the illuminated rooms, even though she must have seen them before and they are not very remarkable.

"*Kirei*," Kazumi keeps saying. "*Kirei, ne?*"

I smile and nod in agreement. I am pleased to be with her and take advantage of the fact that I can squeeze against her with impunity. She gives me no answering pressure when I push my hand against hers—perhaps she imagines that I have done so unintentionally; she does not respond when I put my arm round her deliciously slim waist; she may think that I am protecting her from the crush.

"I must have some sort of a drink soon," I say. "I simply can't stand this much longer."

"Don't you want to go to the Gion Shrine?"

"Oh yes, of course," I reply, lukewarmly.

"It is the shrine of the festival."

"I know."

"We must go."

I agree because I want to please her. We struggle out of the residential quarter, down Shijo Street, past the shrine cars, in which the youths are still inexhaustibly clanging and whining, across Kawaramachi, the bridge, and then up the brilliantly floodlighted portal of the Gion Shrine, whose steep steps are bustling with people ascending and descending. While Kazumi and I are drinking Coca-Cola (not the sort of drink I had meant to have) at a stall in a lantern-lit path that leads up to the shrine buildings, a woman in kimono shyly approaches me.

"Mr. Meadowes, do you remember me?"

"Of course," I lie, trying to recall the name of this pale, plain woman who covers her mouth with a hand.

"Goto Shizu, your student, don't you remember?"

"Ah, yes, Miss Goto!" I do remember her now. She was one of my students during my first year in Japan, one of my best students, and one of my shyest. "What are you doing in Kyoto?"

"I live here."

"Oh yes. I am here for the summer. I have taken Mr. Simpson's house, do you know it? Near the Heian Shrine—"

"No."

Hoping to make Kazumi jealous and hence accommodating, I give Miss Goto my telephone number. My strategy seems to work immediately, for as soon as Miss Goto is out of earshot, Kazumi says sharply, "Who is that?"

"One of my old students."

"You like her?"

"Enormously."

"She is not beautiful."

"She's immensely intelligent."

"You will see her?"

"I hope so."

We wander in silence about the courtyard of the shrine that is ablaze with lanterns. At the main building Kazumi throws a coin into a large wooden receptacle, claps her hands twice, takes hold of the thick rope that hangs down by a gong, flips the rope, and mutters a prayer. I do not copy her, for although her action is not much different from throwing a coin into a fountain or bowing to the new moon and there would be no objection to a foreigner doing it, I should feel an impostor applauding and sounding the gong. We leave the shrine by the upper path that takes us into Maruyama Park, which is ill lit and offers endless opportunity to the would-be seducer, there being many dark corners, benches under trees, walks down sheltered glens. I put my arm round her waist again. It is allowed to remain for a moment, but then Kazumi disengages herself in the act of stumbling over a loose stone; she does this so naturally that I don't know if she has tripped on purpose or not. In any case after the stumble it is time to go home, and we do, to our separate bedrooms.

13

Kazumi has a holiday because of the Gion Festival. It is a very hot day so we watch the procession, which is slow and tedious, on television. The cumbersome shrine cars have fixed wheels and require a laborious lugging round the corners by the scantily clothed pullers, who wipe their sweating bodies with cloths. I find I look at Kazumi more than the screen and she keeps catching my stare; our eyes meet and we are both embarrassed. I go upstairs and sit at my desk and wonder if I should go out and buy Kazumi a pearl brooch.

Because of the festival I decide to stay in and do some work on the Chinese philosophers. The bean-curd man's three-noted horn interrupts my chain of thought. He passes down our lane several times a day. I've seen him once or twice. He is old, with a straw hat that is ocher with age, and he rides a tricycle with a wooden box containing the tofu at the back. His bulb horn reminds me of the musical klaxon of one of my father's motorcars in prewar days when I was a child. I used to think the horn rather superior, especially when it made people look at us. It is strange how this old bean-curd man cycling round Kyoto should be responsible for wafting my mind back to that large touring car of my father's and making me think of Brockenhurst where I was brought up. Whenever I hear this squeaky tootle, I am off in the New Forest for a "run" in the days when motoring was a pleasure, and for me, at the age of seven, an adventure.

The bean-curd hoot becomes distant and I try to concentrate on Li Ho, who in turn sets my mind back on to Kazumi and Noriko, for this T'ang poet and philosopher writes so much about love. "Love, like death, is the most serious event in life," he said. "It shapes not only man's way of life but also his outlook on the world. The human heart subsists on love as does the human body on food. Although love is the highest manifestation of human relationship it is so unstable and insecure that its permanence is always questionable."

I must get Noriko to read this, but either she would not understand or not want to understand.

Once when I was in bed in Tokyo with flu, I gave Noriko a lecture about the impermanence of love. My being ill and having a temperature put me at an advantage; the fever allowed me to speak my mind. I told her bluntly that my love for her had died, that I no longer desired her, that I now regarded her as a friend, and that this was really a great compliment, for friendship lasted longer than a connection based on passion. "You have been promoted to the rank of friend," I said, feigning emotion in a hoarse voice. "It is a great honor." Had I not had a highish temperature I could never have uttered such nonsense without laughing. She sat in a chair at the other side of the room (I would not let her come near me in spite of her plea that she didn't mind catching my cold as it was mine) and stared at me with doe eyes, nodding from time to time. I was pleased with the reception my remarks were getting and at the end I was sure that I had succeeded in bringing the affair to a close.

"Do you understand?" I asked, when my peroration on the transience of love and the permanence of friendship was over.

"Yes."

"Good."

She rose and approached my bed.

"NO!" I screamed, hysterically. "Don't come near me!"

She stopped halfway between the chair and the bed. Her face wore an expression of alarm.

"Goodbye, then," she said solemnly.

I felt that I had been cruel and had gone too far. "I want to see you often. You know that."

"Yes." She stood rooted to the floor.

I put my hand on my forehead and groaned. "You'd better leave now. I think I should try and sleep a bit, if I am to avoid a serious relapse."

She went to the door, opened it and loudly said, as if declaiming, "I love you!" and was gone.

While I am here musing about Li Ho, the bean-curd man, and my father's Bentley, Kazumi calls me to the telephone, which I should not have answered had I been alone in the house.

It is Miss Goto.

"Thank you very much for your kindness yesterday."

For a moment I wonder what she means, for we had simply exchanged a few words at the shrine; I had done nothing for her. "It was a pleasure to see you," I say.

"I have a plan for your sightseeing of Kyoto."

"Oh?" I don't want such a plan. I don't want to be made to see things. But somehow Miss Goto interests me and has done so ever since she was my student—is it her intellectuality, her gentleness, her extreme diffidence, or her humility? Perhaps it is the last attribute; she would be easy to handle. "It's very kind of you. Would you like to come to tea tomorrow and we can discuss plans?"

She agrees and I arrange to meet her at the bus stop on the corner.

Kazumi seems suspicious. She says, "You are going to meet her?"

"She's coming to tea tomorrow."

"Tea? Afternoon tea? Very English," Kazumi retorts scornfully.

Can it be that Kazumi is jealous? How can she be if she has no interest in me? Perhaps I have played my cards well.

Kazumi and I spend the day indoors, except for a short shopping expedition on which I accompany her, and all the time I feel she would rather be on her own. She is well-acquainted with the shop-keepers, who now know me, and I sense that my being with her solves the riddle that has been in their minds. The woman in the butcher's shop seems to give me a knowing look, as if to say, "Now I understand why you have come to spend the hot summer in Kyoto," and the young man in the grocer's eyes me quizzically, says something to the girl assistant who glances in my direction, and sniggers. Such is my impression, but I may well be wrong; it is easy for a foreigner to misinterpret a Japanese regard, a Japanese smile. At each shop Kazumi exclaims like every Japanese in summertime, "*Atsui desu ne!*" ("Hot, isn't it?") and without fail the reply comes, "*So desu ne!*" ("Yes it is, isn't it?").

Kazumi is armed with a plastic shopping basket like any conventional housewife, and she fits perfectly into the scene of swarming women in the narrow, covered market, while I feel out of place. In a chemist's shop, where I buy some toothpaste, she flops into a chair by an electric fan and orders a little bottle of a vitamin drink which she sucks up with a straw.

"I'll have one too," I say.

"It's very, very—how shall I say?"

"Efficacious."

How hypocritical of me! If Noriko and not Kazumi were sitting in the torrid shop sucking up the ridiculous vitamin stuff, I should have been skeptical; I should have chaffed her for being a dupe to the TV advertisers. As it is I imbibe my vitamin liquid with affected relish.

"Effie what?" asks Kazumi.

"Efficacious. It means having the desired effect."

She laughs and says, "I see," but I don't think she does see the point.

Kazumi says she wants to cook the dinner for a change, so to please her I agree. In the depths of the market she buys (with money I have given her) four bits of chicken from a tiny shop, a hole-in-the-wall place whose two rough and roguish-looking assistants, unshaven and with kerchiefs round their heads, specialize in selling cut-up birds. The assistants joke with Kazumi, bawdily, I think, but I don't understand.

When Kazumi produces her concoction, fried chicken with mushroom sauce (tinned mushrooms mixed into a rather lumpy Béchamel), I am for a few moments in a position of advantage, because being uncertain about the results of her cooking she has lost her customary poise. In order to put her at ease and, I hope, curry favor, I give fulsome praise to the food.

"This is really excellent," I say. "Really excellent. *Oishii.*"

"I am glad," she replies, humbly.

"Absolutely marvelous."

At the end of the meal I put my hands together, bow my head and say, "*Gochisosama.* I forbid you to do the washing up."

And contrary to what I expect, she agrees and leaves me to cope with the plates and the greasy pans, and when, soaked with sweat and exhausted, I go into the sitting room I find her in her TV position, feet stretched out along the bench seat, right hand supporting her head, left hand holding a cigarette, and oblivious to my presence.

14

"I know you have been in Kyoto before, Mr. Meadows," says Miss Goto, "But I should like to show you some special things that I do not think you have seen."

"Oh yes."

"For example, have you seen the morning glory flowers in the Botanical Gardens?"

"No."

"Well then, if we meet at five one morning—"

"At five?"

"At six, then. The flowers or should I say the blooms?"

"Either would do."

"The flowers, then, are at their best in the early morning—"

"Hence their name, I suppose."

With her hand over her mouth, Miss Goto goes into a paroxysm of laughter.

"Have some more tea, Miss Goto."

"No thank you."

"Oh, go on, do! You've only had one cup."

"Thank you very much. I mean, yes, please."

I pour some tea into Miss Goto's cup. She has been perched on the edge of the bench seat for about half an hour politely conversing, often with a hand screening her mouth. Her face is pale and devoid of make-up; her straight, jet hair is done in the simplest way and hangs directly down from the central parting. Two strands of hair, one from each side of her part, occasionally fall over her forehead and her cheeks in the manner of an old-fashioned hairstyle. These strands are the only signs of feminine vanity that Miss Goto allows herself. Her glasses are rimless and give her a severe look; her dress, pink with a black flower pattern, is very much a best dress, and has obviously been cast in that category for several years; her dark-blue and yellow straw handbag is of the wallet kind and comes I know (I got one for Noriko a year or two ago) from the folk-art shop in Kawaramachi.

Perhaps it is because I do not know Miss Goto well that she appears more delicate, more refined, and much more the Westerner's idea of a Japanese lady than either Noriko or Kazumi. Miss Goto is so polite, so deferential, so considerate (she would never lounge about watching television while I was in the kitchen doing the washing up) and—this is what I like most about her—so intelligent and intellectual.

I mention my T'ang poets and not only has she heard of them but she contributes an opinion of her own which is sensible and fresh.

In her quiet, hesitant, and sometimes inaudible voice she tells me about herself like a self-conscious spinster in the confessional. "I am thirty-five years old, Mr. Meadowes," she begins, and noticing my look of surprise she explains, "I did not go to the university until

I was twenty-nine. You see, I could not go while my father was alive as he was old and I had to help my mother look after him."

"Why did you go to the university in Tokyo when your home was in Kyoto?"

"I had spent all my life in Kyoto—you are a foreigner and cannot know how restricting and provincial Kyoto is—and I wanted to spend some years in Tokyo. It had always been my dream to go abroad but that was not possible, nor will it ever be."

"You might get a scholarship, a Fulbright or something."

"I am too old."

"Not for post-graduate study."

"I never graduated."

"Oh yes, of course, I remember now, I was surprised when you didn't turn up in the fourth-year class. You had done so well."

She looked down. "My mother became ill. I had to return here to look after her."

"And now, is she—"

"She is well, but she is old. I cannot leave her."

"You have no other relations who could—?"

"I have only a married sister. She is too busy with her children." After a longish pause, Miss Goto says, "You haven't told me why you came to spend the summer in hot Kyoto."

"I had the offer of this house and I like Kyoto very much."

"Thank you," she replies, as if I had complimented her on her own work. "I hate it."

"But it's such a wonderful city."

"I hate it because it is so provincial; it is like Barchester. You've no idea. The smallness of the people's minds. The citizens of Kyoto are petty and gossipy—can I say gossipy?"

"Yes."

"Thank you. They are gossipy and hypo, hypo, er—"

"Hypocritical?"

"Hypocritical. You see, I forget my English, Mr. Meadowes."

"You remember it well."

"I have no practice now. I recall your frequent use of hypocritical, your explanation of hypocrisy."

"Oh?" I dislike being reminded of my fatuous observations. "I've always found the Kyoto people charming. The shopowners and their assistants in this district, for example, are so—"

"Mr. Meadowes, you are too kind. You, a foreigner, cannot know what living in Kyoto is really like."

She goes on, in a voice that is almost passionate, to complain that she does not require any English for her clerical work in a hospital, and she dismisses my suggestion that her knowledge of Wordsworth might provide private pleasure. She stresses, rather, melodramatically, that she is like a person who has been promised freedom and then denied it, that learning English literature and European history was an escape, but it was also frustrating, being similar to reading a book on swimming and never being allowed near water. "Here in Kyoto," she concluded, "in little Kyoto—you may think it is a big city but it is not, Mr. Meadowes—I feel in a trap; limited; sentenced to life imprisonment."

"Really, Miss Goto, it can't be so bad as that! With your intelligence you can surely find solace in reading. Think of Jane Austen, she—"

"Excuse me, Mr. Meadowes, I know what you are going to say. You told us about Jane Austen in one of your classes."

"Oh dear, what an awful thing it is to be a teacher! Especially one whose students are blessed with good memories."

"I am sorry, Mr. Meadowes."

Miss Goto looks at her hands, folded together on her lap; she turns her left wrist so the face of her little round silver watch is within sight. "Oh!" she exclaims, apparently astonished. "I must be going."

"Do stay a bit longer. I so enjoy chatting with you."

"Mr. Meadowes, I am very sorry." She still regards her hands as if ashamed; she has changed from the Western-educated student, which she has been for a short while, to demure Japanese spinster.

"What about?"

"I must apologize. I have been very impolite."

"No, you haven't."

"I have," she insists. "I was very rude to ramble on about myself as I did."

"No, you weren't."

"I was." She seems to desire self-abasement. "I can't help it.

Once I start talking about myself I let myself go and"—her head drops lower so only the top of it is visible—"I do not have much chance to say what I feel."

"Miss Goto," I say, firmly, "Please understand that you have been neither rude nor impolite, that there is not the slightest need to apologize for anything. Would you like a drink?"

"Oh no, thank you. I must be running along."

I accompany her to the bus stop at the corner. She at once answers my question about the temple opposite my house, telling me it is called Honmyo-ji and that it belongs to the Nichiren sect.

"It is not an important temple. Thank you very much, Mr. Meadowes. Some day, when you are not so busy, perhaps you will let me show you an interesting sight? Goodbye."

15 I go to the barber's shop on the corner by the bus stop and surrender my head to the solicitous and skillful hands of a young hairdresser, whose own locks straggle untidily down to his shoulders. In other lands I hate having my hair cut, but in Japan I enjoy it, for the barbers are careful and thorough, and never hint that they wish to finish hurriedly in order to get on with the next customer. The barbers don't talk unless they are addressed, their fingers are not nicotine stained, and their breath does not smell. They do this very personal and rather revolting task as self-effacingly as possible.

While the young man painstakingly snips at the back of my neck, I frown at my reflection in the mirror. How gross and self-indulgent I look! I stare at myself and wonder what Miss Goto thinks of me. Could she, I ask myself, putting my chin in the air, like me? The barber, gently, almost apologetically, pushes my head down. The snip-snip rhythm of the scissors sends my mind maundering into imaginary scenes with Miss Goto. She is duly impressed and greatly appreciative of the dinner I give her at the Kyoto Hotel; she intelligently translates the Japanese subtitles of a Swedish film which we see together and discuss at length afterwards. I lend her

some of my poems and she praises them and offers some construc-
tive suggestions, a thing which my wife has never done, and which
Noriko and Kazumi are incapable of doing. By the time my hair has
been cut and the barber is voluptuously rubbing soap into my head, I
have compared Miss Goto with the three other women in my life
and she has come out best. Miss Goto's English is nearly perfect; she
can understand everything I say and she knows enough about English literature and English history to feel at ease with English people; she would never become argumentative or difficult like an
English wife; she would always defer. I should be the senior partner
as a man ought to be, not an equal, nor, as I feel with my wife, a
junior partner or, at times, an inferior employee of the firm. Also,
Miss Goto would remain Japanese and not try to become English or
emulate me as does Noriko.

I lie right back in the barber's chair with a soothing hot towel
over my face and begin to think that Kazumi and Miss Goto would
be different from Noriko, especially Miss Goto. Noriko is from the
middle class and therefore petty and limited; Kazumi, whose origins
are working class, and Miss Goto, whose manners and deportment
suggest an aristocratic background or at least an old-fashioned one,
would be less irritating. As the young barber kneads the back of my
neck with his supple fingers and then pummels the area around my
shoulder blades, I try to imagine what Kazumi and Miss Goto would
be like in England. I decide that, although Kazumi might keep me in
a state of uncertainty by flirting with my friends (and possibly such a
state is an exciting one to be in), Miss Goto would be loyal and
intelligent and that these qualities are what one most desires.

16

The girls' school across the road has broken
up for the holidays, but the school band seems
to have decided to spend the summer practicing. All the morning I am subjected to do-re-
mi being played slowly and deliberately, with
a pause between each ragged chord. The
rainy season is over and it is much hotter. While walking back from

the shops at noon yesterday I felt quite dizzy from the scorching sun.

Kazumi has decided to go to her apartment this weekend while Noriko is here. This is bad, for it means that Noriko will want to share my bed and I don't want her to. Kazumi has, though, promised to attend the dinner party I am giving on Friday and Bob Watkins has also accepted my invitation and as usual refused for his wife. I had thought of asking Miss Goto but then I decided not to. I don't want her to know about my other friends. Kazumi says that she will come back to stay on Monday after Noriko has gone. I wish I could sleep right through till Monday.

After lunch, in the heat of the day, I take a taxi to Kyoto Station to meet Noriko. On the way I feel pleased at the thought of seeing her, but as soon as I sight the blue and white train coming relentlessly into the platform my heart sinks.

"Hello, darling!"

I don't know why exactly but the way Noriko pronounces "darling" makes me writhe; for some reason it sounds unnatural on her lips, and silly, and she seems to succeed in saying it in a smug way that I find irritating. So my feelings in the taxi back to the house are those of boredom at the thought of the weekend, the long weekend—it is only Friday.

"I can stay till Monday, darling."

"Don't you have to be at work on Monday morning?"

"It doesn't matter."

I can think of absolutely nothing to say and we drive past Higashi Honganji in silence. Going down Shijo Street, Noriko speaks.

"Will she be there?"

"Not for tonight, but she's coming to dinner. I've also asked Professor Watkins, so we'll be four."

"I see." Noriko remains glum until we reach the house. "It's very hot, isn't it?" She fans her face ineffectively with a small, folded handkerchief, while I fiddle with the door key.

"There's an air conditioner." I slide open the door.

"In the bedroom?" she inquires, as she is slipping off her shoes in the *genkan*.

"No, only in here." We enter the sitting room. She flings her arms round my neck and kisses me.

"I must hurry," I say, extricating myself from her warm embrace. "There's dinner to prepare. In about two hours Professor Watkins and Kazumi-san will be here."

"May I help you?"

"Yes, but let me show you your room first."

I fetch her bag from the *genkan* and lead her along the dark passage to the downstairs moon-viewing room, which is exceedingly hot.

"I'm afraid this room has no mosquito screens, but you can light the anti-mosquito stuff; it lasts most of the night."

Her disappointment is manifest. "You do not sleep here?"

"I sleep in the room on the other side of the house. It's too hot to share a bed."

"I see." She looks tired; her brown eyes look tired. She has often complained about the smallness of her eyes; big eyes are admired in Japan.

"There's a host of things to do for the party tonight. Will you help me?"

"Of course, darling."

Her willingness rather puts my brusqueness to shame. She comes to the kitchen and peels potatoes and scrapes carrots without a murmur.

While arranging chrysanthemums in the cool of the sitting room, I wish that I still found Noriko attractive; it would make life so much simpler if I did.

Before the guests are due, Noriko reminds me that she wants to go to Arashiyama, where we went together four years ago. It's a pleasant, much-frequented spot with temples, a river, steep tree-covered hills; it has been altogether ruined by the souvenir shops, restaurants, cafes, bars, and small hotels that now blight the place. To avoid argument and to ensure she'll go on helping in the kitchen, I say, "We'll go Sunday, shall we?"

Noriko kisses me again.

17

Bob and I are having drinks before dinner. Noriko and Kazumi are in the kitchen preparing the meal, almost vying with each other in their efforts to help. I am on edge wondering what the girls are saying. On her arrival this evening Kazumi kissed me in the genkan, just before Noriko noisily appeared to see who had come, and I'm not sure if she saw or not. Noriko is overplaying the part of "wife" of the house.

When Bob arrived Kazumi cooed at him like an enamored dove. Her voice went high and she said, "*Shibaraku ne!*" ("It's been a long time, hasn't it?") about five times. Bob seemed delighted with this effusive welcome. He took both her hands in his and held them for a few moments. "It's sure good to see you, Kazumi-san." After more coos and exclamations of joy, Bob came into the sitting room and Kazumi rejoined Noriko in the kitchen.

"Well, Bob, how's the play going?" I am not in the least interested in the wretched drama festival in which Bob and his students participate but I know it is dear to his heart.

"Fine, fine! We're doing *Kagotsurube*, you know the Kabuki play?"

"I may, but I can never remember the titles of the Kabuki plays I've seen."

"It's about a rich, pockmarked farmer who goes to the pleasure quarter in Edo and falls for one of the leading courtesans."

"Oh yes, I know it. Are you doing it in Japanese?"

"No, no, in English. But with proper Japanese costumes, make-up, and gestures. Hope you're going to be here for it."

"I should be."

"Good."

"Have another drink!"

Bob hands me his glass, which I take with mine into the kitchen, where Noriko and Kazumi are working in silence.

"More whiskey, *darling?*"

"Please."

"Ice, *darling?*"

"Please."

I don't like these pointed "darlings" said in front of Kazumi on purpose. If I were Japanese, Noriko would never be so familiar in front of a third person.

Noriko scuttles to the refrigerator and while she is pulling out one of the ice trays Kazumi gives me another kiss. I find this second kiss given literally behind Noriko's back and a yard away from her curiously exciting, but I cannot understand why, now that Noriko is here, Kazumi starts this coquettish behavior.

I return to the sitting room.

"Dinner won't be long," I say.

"I'm in no hurry," returns Bob. "Is Kazumi-san staying here now that your little friend has come?"

"No. She's staying in her *apato*."

"Her decision or yours?" Bob asks in the manner of a needling teacher; for a moment I visualize him in the classroom trying to make silent, shy Japanese students reply to his questions.

"Hers, actually. I would have liked her to stay."

Bob raises his eyebrows.

"As a companion to Noriko. I'm busy scribbling much of the day." Bob eyes me quizzically and I betray my dislike of his inquisitiveness by abruptly changing the subject. "D'you have to attend faculty meetings?" I ask, fatuously.

"Yeah. Been going for twenty years now. Why?"

"I just wondered. I don't, thank God. The meetings are held about once a week, and the most trivial subjects are discussed, apparently. The other day I was told that the professors discussed whether colored chalks should be used. It was suggested that yellow should be banned as it did not show up very well. But not everyone agreed. Some pointed out that since the blackboards were green, yellow showed up better than white. Others complained that colored chalks dirtied the fingers more than white. The discussion went on for hours and no decision was reached. Can you imagine anything so absurd as to waste the time of professors with such trivialities?"

"Yeah," says Bob, flatly, "I can easily, and not only in Japan."

Noriko appears. "Dinner ready."

I place Bob on my left, Kazumi on my right, and Noriko opposite me at the other end of the table.

Noriko has placed the bowls of Vichyssoisse (not from a tin) round the table. I say, "*Dozo*," the others say, "*Itadakimasu*," and we begin to eat.

A silence follows which Bob and I break at the same time. I say to him, "How's your—," and he says to Noriko, "So you live in—," we both say, "Sorry," I say, "Please go ahead, Bob."

"So you live in Tokyo, Noriko-san?"

"Yes."

Silence again.

"What were you going to say, Peter?" asks Bob.

I was going to ask him how his wife was, but I now feel it's better not to mention her for he might ask me how mine is, so I say, "I forget now."

"Couldn't have been very important."

"No."

Noriko rises and collects the soup bowls. Bob seems to be leaning forwards slightly and so does Kazumi. I have an idea that they are holding hands under the table, but I can't bend down and look. Noriko reappears and puts the casserole of *daube de boeuf* in front of me so I can serve it. I notice that Bob and Kazumi straighten their backs as if they have released their hands. Noriko fetches the vegetables, puts them in the middle of the table, and regains her place. She really serves very well and with more training could be a good cook. If only I could take her to England as a maid and that she would remain in that status!

Silence as we start our stew.

They say solemnly in chorus, "*Oishii!*" and go on eating. I pour out the wine: French *vin de table*, not expensive.

I say, "Noriko and I are going to Arashiyama on Sunday, would you like to come?"

Noriko stares at me. I know she wants us to go alone.

"Can't. Rehearsal," replies Bob.

"And you Kazumi-san?"

"I am sorry. I must see my sister in Osaka."

A lie?

Silence while we continue to eat our stew. I stretch out my leg and like an antenna my socked foot searches and then touches Bob's socked foot, which is on top of Kazumi's stockinged foot, I think, for he pulls his foot away and so does she. "Sorry," I say, letting out an

involuntary laugh. Bob throws me a glare which I interpret as meaning, "Don't interfere."

I say for perhaps the first time in my life, "Anything good on
television tonight?"

"Never look at the darned thing."

Noriko replies, "Yamamura Saburo is on tonight," putting his
first name last in the Japanese way.

"Everyone's pet," I say. "Housewives, their daughters, they're all
in love with him."

"And the gays too, I guess," puts in Bob, sourly.

"Kazumi adores him," I declare.

Kazumi blushes. "He is a good singer."

The next course is an orange soufflé, a recipe from Elizabeth
David's *Mediterranean Food*. Bob pushes his helping aside. "No sweets
for me," he says and lights a cigarette. I wish we were at my London
club, where smoking is prohibited in the dining room.

We move to the sitting room and after about three-quarters of
an hour of desultory conversation Bob rises and says, "*Domo
gochisosama deshita*," and then to Kazumi, "You coming?"

Kazumi gets up like an obedient child, bows uttering the same
idiot compliment about "it having been a feast," and leaves with
Bob.

For the rest of the evening, while Noriko has her eyes glued to
the television set, I wonder whether Bob is rolling about on the
tatami of Kazumi's flat.

Noriko and I retire to our separate bedrooms.

18 One of Noriko's good characteristics, and
one I shamefully exploit, is that she never
encourages me to be extravagant, and will-
ingly accepts an economy. Noriko and I go by
bus to Omiya Station on the other side of the
city, and then we take the crowded tram-
train to Arashiyama. I should not have dared suggest such forms of
transport to Kazumi; one only spoils those whom one desires.

Timid and delicate though Japanese women may look in repose, while traveling they become tough and uncompromising; with arms bent and elbows out they nip onto a train more quickly than most men and they are less particular than the stronger sex about queue priorities. Noriko is as good at these tactics as any Japanese female, and at Omiya Station after buying our tickets from a slot machine she insinuates her way up the queue and secures two seats on the tram-train to Arashiyama. I call it a tram-train for at one moment it has a line fenced in like a proper railway, and at the next it is careering down the middle of a street.

"We get out here," says Noriko, rising.

"But this is not Arashiyama."

"We must see Koryuji temple," she replies, edging her way through the tightly packed passengers, many of whom are young and brightly clad in summer garb. Their mood is bright too. Others are getting out at this stop, a popular one for sightseers. There is no place for another body in the crowded tram, so if one body moves another must take its place. I ooze out onto the platform behind a desperate mother whose children have gone ahead, burrowing through the passengers' legs like ferrets.

"Why," I say to Noriko, who manages somehow to look fairly cool. "Why get out here?"

"To see Koryuji."

"I don't want to see it again."

"But we see it last time."

Noriko is determined to repeat exactly our visit of four years ago. I grunt and grumpily walk with her along the temple paths. We glance at the twelfth-century Lecture Hall, designated an Important Cultural Property, and the second oldest building in Kyoto, but being of wood one presumes that the pillars, beams, and floorboards have been replaced now and then over the years. The temple, though, was founded in the seventh century for the repose of the soul of the great Prince Shotoku, who propagated Buddhism in Japan and gave the country a constitution. One knows him well, for his likeness appears on banknotes and there is a statue of him in this temple according to the guide book, but it is not on view. The main reason, I think, for Noriko wanting to revisit this temple is because of a seventh-century statue of a bodhisattva reputed to be the oldest piece of sculpture in Kyoto and designated as National Treasure Number One. It indeed deserves to be a national treasure, this elegant, rather feminine figure, which leans slightly forward, the third finger of its right hand joined to the thumb and the long middle finger almost touching the cheek, the little finger erect—the position of the fingers is supposed to indicate deep thought. The middle finger was too tempting for a schoolboy some years ago and he broke it off. Noriko reminds me of this act of vandalism as she did before. The finger has been repaired, of course, and the statue is now out of reach, protected by a glass wall. "They move it back," says Noriko, after striking a copper bell with the stick by its side, putting her hands together and saying a little prayer.

"I can understand that schoolboy who broke off the finger," I say. "Somehow it's provocative."

"Come along, Peter," calls Noriko, imitating me. I have often given her a similar command. I obey and we crunch our way down the hot, stony paths back to the station.

"I am glad to see the statue again," declares Noriko.

"Why?"

"Because it is beautiful and because I see it twice and twice with you."

"I don't see the connection."

"Oh Peter!"

We squeeze onto another tram and at last reach Arashiyama. On our previous visit to this popular beauty spot we hired a room in an exclusive old-fashioned restaurant that hides itself among the pines, the maples, and the cherry trees and is some distance from the souvenir shops, the noodle shops, the bars, and the cafes.

Noriko goes down to a wooden building by the river and begins to speak to a clerk.

"No," I protest.

"Yes," she insists and arranges to hire a boat.

We walk along a plank across the small pebbly beach and get into a flat-bottomed boat which is partly roofed with green corrugated iron. The boat has no seats, but on the floor is a mat with a red rug on top of it. We take off our shoes and sit in the stern. The boatman stands in the pointed bow and punts us upstream. The river is wide at this point and there are many rowing boats and others like ours dotted about the expanse of calm water; wails about lost love from transistors and the restaurants along the shore tear the air.

"We can't go to that restaurant," I say.

"Why?"

"We haven't told them we're coming. You know it's the sort of place one has to warn in advance."

"Let us try." Noriko is quite determined. Soft-hearted, loving though she be, once she has decided on what she wants she sets out to get it. This was true when we first met that day on the train where fate placed us next to each other on the bullet express from Kyoto to Tokyo. I had only a few days left and had not intended to stay in Japan, but I did because of Noriko. She had fallen so completely in love with me that it went to my head. Never had I been so loved. Now when I look back on those first mad weeks of our affair, I can see how her relentless love worked on me. Its relentlessness is still there, but I resist it since it no longer bowls me over. Today, though, I have decided to let Noriko have her way. Her steadfast love and loyalty deserve occasional reward. Today is prize day.

We lean against the square back of the boat with our legs stretched out in front of us. The roof intervenes between us and the boatman, who is punting in the bow. Noriko puts her hand on mine. "This is lovely," she says. "This memory day."

We land and dismiss the boatman. We have not gone far, only about a quarter of a mile in fact, but we have passed all the restaurants and cafes, and now after climbing a ladder we walk along the bank. We go up the rough stone steps and come to the little restaurant which is like an old-fashioned Japanese house. We tinkle the bell and a lady in kimono appears and tells us very politely that she cannot cope with unexpected visitors. I do not say "I told you so" to Noriko, who, surprisingly, is undeterred by the rebuff. She takes my hand and leads me to an open space among the tall, slanting pines where there is a cafe, piped music, and a rather open lavatory, and then up a narrow path that climbs a hill. We come to a clearing where young men and girls are playing games. Noriko releases my hand. She is still shy of her compatriots seeing that we are lovers, although the fact that we are together suggests that this is so. The foliage is thick on either side of the path and sometimes a branch slaps our faces. "*Itai, itai!*" ("It hurts!"), Noriko exclaims childishly.

At the top of the hill, there are pines and views of the mountain on the other side of the river, the distant city, the river upstream.

Noriko takes my hand again and leads me up a narrower and more overgrown path and when we come to a tiny sward she stops and throws her arms round my neck.

"It was here," she says, triumphantly. She has remembered the place of our lovemaking four years ago. "Please," she adds, pulling me to the ground.

"What about all those people?" Their shouts and shrieks sound near.

"They not come here." We are kneeling opposite one another. She pulls me over on top of her.

"No!" I protest.

Her dexterous fingers encourage my desire, which is for some reason increased by the fact that the voices of the young trippers are audible and perhaps because of the possibility of being discovered by them. The risk of discovery excites and with Kazumi in my mind's eye I briefly and selfishly perform the act of lust.

19 I am sitting at my desk in the bedroom with the fan trained on my back. I have just returned from seeing Noriko off at the station. I am thankful she has gone and there is no danger of her reappearing until the end of August. Today is Monday, only the third of the month, and Kazumi is supposed to return here this evening. She has not telephoned, but she promised to come in time for dinner. I must cook her a special meal. It is hotter. The highest temperature yesterday when Noriko and I were at Arashiyama was ninety-four degrees and today is just as hot, if not hotter. In spite of the heat, the girls' school band is groaning up and down the scale.

I regret having made love to Noriko yesterday afternoon because I have probably revived her hopes more than I have done for months, although as soon as it was over I did my best to dampen them by behaving boorishly. It was the first time for about a year.

The last occasion was in a Japanese inn at a small town on the west coast; as yesterday, it was on a scorching afternoon and, I remember well, the sliding door was open so that anyone on the landing could have seen us.

I behaved badly on our return from Arashiyama yesterday, forbidding Noriko to sleep in my bed, and this morning she was sweet to me, getting breakfast ready, ironing two pairs of my trousers, and sewing on some shirt buttons. Now, as usual when she has just left me, I feel I ought to have been nicer, and also I feel ashamed about my brutish behavior at Arashiyama and last night.

The band tumbles down the scale raggedly. The girls have not made much progress this morning and they have to compete with three cicadas in the paulownia tree outside the south window. These insects work themselves up into a screaming noise like a factory machine going at full blast, then they slow down and croak intermittently.

I open my notebook and stare at the sentence I wrote a few days ago about this confounded poet Li Ho: "Love like death is the most serious event in life. It shapes not only man's way of life but also his outlook on the world." The second part of this statement is true enough, but Li Ho should have included the aftereffects of love, for this morning was black until Noriko's train pulled out of the station; now the thought of Kazumi coming tonight has brightened the horizon somewhat. I say somewhat because I vaguely suspect her of giving in to Bob's blandishments, and it probably wasn't for the first time. What shall I give her for dinner? After some perusal of the cookery books I decide on risotto for she praised that dish highly the last time I gave it to her, and it is easy to make except that it means a struggle out in the heat to buy chicken livers.

I put on my shoes and walk to the market. It is stupendously hot; nevertheless, the girls have not given up blowing their trumpets and their trombones in spite of the fact that they are in a room without either air conditioning or a fan. I buy chicken livers at a shop that is nearer than the one Kazumi went to—did she go to the farther shop because she likes the men there? I return home and spend the rest of the afternoon in the air-conditioned room. The bedroom is so hot in the afternoon, even with the fan full on, and downstairs the girls' band is muted by the close window. I lie on the bench seat cogitating on the hypothesis that the kisses which Kazumi gave me while Noriko was here mean that she doesn't find me repulsive. But why did she flirt with Bob or allow him to flirt with her?

At four o'clock, for want of something better to do, I ring up Miss Goto. She seems pleased to hear from me and suggests calling tomorrow to take me on a "surprise" tour. I agree. At five-thirty I begin to prepare the risotto. At six-thirty the risotto is ready but Kazumi has not come in. I pour myself a large whiskey and begin to worry and to feel lonely. At six-forty I remember that Kazumi hasn't a key because I borrowed hers for Noriko, so I go to the front door and look out, both ways. The woman opposite is standing in her doorway. I jerk a bow at her and retreat. I imagine that there is a certain amount of gossip among the housewives about me and seeing me waiting in the doorway for Kazumi might set tongues wagging.

As soon as I hear the front door rattle open and Kazumi's cry of "*Tadaima*," I hurry to the *genkan* step.

"How nice to see you!" For some reason I am shy and rather formal.

"Sorry to be late."

"Never mind."

She is hot but not more so than I after my activities in the kitchen, going to the front door and back, drinking whiskey. "Would you like a shower before supper?"

"If it's all right."

"Of course."

"Are you sure?"

"Perfectly." It is as if we were strangers.

When we are sitting at the dining table, with our legs in the hole, eating the risotto (about which she says, "*Oishii!*") I press my knee against hers and while she does not move away she does not return the pressure. Why? What was the meaning of the kisses she gave me when Noriko was here? I rack my brains to try and recall anything I could possibly have done to offend her when she was last in the house, an exercise one finds oneself constantly performing in Japan. The last time she was here was at the dinner party for Bob and I can't remember doing anything except discover Bob's foot on top of hers under the dining table, and I did this unintentionally, and reciprocate when she kissed me. Perhaps she's slightly put out because she thinks I suspect her and Bob of being lovers. I wonder if Bob did go to her flat. Will I ever know?

The telephone rings. I know it is Noriko before I have picked up the receiver.

"Hello," she says, uncertainly as if she expected me to be angry with her for telephoning.

After a pause, I say, "Did you have a good journey?"

"Yes, all right, thank you."

"Good."

We then observe our telephone silence as there is nothing I want to say. There are lots of things I could say; I could refer to our day at Arashiyama, or thank her for helping in the house ("Your being here made all the difference. . . ." that sort of thing) or express the hope that she come down again soon.

"Is *she* there?"

I know she means Kazumi, but I reply, "Who?"

"Kazumi-san."

I hesitate wondering whether I should lie or not. "Yes, she is here."

"May I speak to her, please?"

Ill-temperedly, I say, "Yes, if you want to."

Kazumi and Noriko speak for almost ten minutes and I cannot grasp what they are saying for Kazumi only utters an occasional "*So desu ne!*" But when the conversation is over, Kazumi says to me, "Noriko-san is jealous. She thinks you and me are lovers."

"She's wrong though, isn't she?"

"She loves you very much."

I grunt.

Kazumi offers to do the washing up and I do not help her for I am displeased that the two women should have discussed me on the telephone, as no doubt they have; and with me sitting a yard away. I feel they have formed a sort of pact whereby Kazumi has promised not to succumb to my charms.

The TV set is switched on as soon as she comes from the kitchen. It is a "Sabu-chan" night—it would be! This evening Saburo Yamamura looks more adult, for he is wearing a dinner jacket instead of teenage clothes. As usual he dances badly and sings worse, this time in front of six male dancers in bellboy uniforms who wave their arms in a nervous, agitated manner, like automata whose mechanism is moving at twice the speed it is meant to.

I scoff. "Absurd."

"I don't think so," says Kazumi.

"I do. I'm going upstairs."

No reply.

"I'm going upstairs."

"To bed?"

"Probably." I get no reaction. "Good night."

"*Oyasumi nasai.*"

In bed I read *Fanny Hill* and think about Miss Goto, who is better mannered, I'm sure, than either Kazumi or Noriko. The clacking sticks go on for about three-quarters of an hour and keep me awake when I am ready to sleep.

20

I am awakened by shouts and the clatter of doors and windows sliding open. From my bed I watch the woman in the house opposite removing the windows of the upstairs room and taking them inside—if unlocked, the windows of a Japanese-style house can be lifted out with ease. I go downstairs and look into the lane. The occupants of every household are removing their doors and their windows and taking out their tatami. Has there been some sort of earthquake warning? Are people folding up their houses and abandoning the district? Kazumi, who is in the kitchen, tells me it is our lane's day for the annual "clean," the *osoji,* when all households clean their houses.

"Shall we have to clean our house?"

"No."

"Will it matter if we don't?"

"No. This is foreigner's house."

I fear, though, that we will be branded as the lane's dirty-house–householders and perhaps the local house committee (I believe there is one) will organize a demonstration against me or throw stones at the paper windows. I tell all this to Miss Goto, who comes punctually at ten o'clock to take me on our "surprise" tour, but she doesn't realize I am joking.

"I don't think there is any danger, Mr. Meadowes," she says, solemnly.

And my laughter in reply makes her look confused.

Miss Goto and I leave the house soon after her arrival and we are roasted on the corner for several long minutes before getting a taxi. She suggests going by bus, but I refuse and I don't think she is sorry. The Municipal Library at the far end of the city is the first "surprise" that Miss Goto has in store for me. The library building is modern and light and spacious, though not cool. Round the sides of the exhibition room is a special show of scroll pictures and in the glass cases in the middle are old kimonos. Ghost stories make one shiver with fear and are therefore, according to Japanese tradition, cooling, so ghost plays are put on in July and August.

All the scrolls are pictures of ghosts, some of which are extremely gruesome. I feign horror by putting a hand over my eyes and turning away after glancing at a woman with blood streaming from her mouth and in whose hands is a severed head (did she bite it off?). Miss Goto, I think, fears I am going to faint for she takes my elbow and steers me away from the wall to look at an eighteenth-century summer kimono, which is faded and moth-eaten.

"I am sorry," she says, taking on full responsibility for the grisly scrolls.

We revive our shattered nerves with iced coffee in the cafeteria and then we stand hotly in the road waiting for a taxi.

The next "surprise" is the Zen temple, Nanzenji, which is near my house and familiar, but I have not seen its subsidiary temple, Konchi-in, and am pleased to do so, though I wonder why she didn't take me here first. In an apologetic whisper Miss Goto tells me about the temple while I gaze at the fat carp swimming in the pond just inside the entrance. "Founded in 1400 by Shogun Yoshimichi Ashikaga—" The noise of the cicadas drowns the quiet voice. She leads me up a narrow path through a gate, up some steps to another

gate where we present our tickets to an old man sitting in a kind of
sentry box, and then she mutters to me about the Toshogu Shrine, a
Shinto affair built in 1628 in accordance with the will of Ieyasu
Tokugawa, the first of the Tokugawa shoguns. "You will notice that
the painted carvings—the peacocks and the peonies—are similar to
those at the shrine at Nikko, though less gorgeous. . . ."

"You ought to be a guide."

"I am one in my spare time."

"I mean you explain so well, much better than a guide would.
Guides are usually ghastly—I mean most guides, of course. . . ." I
keep putting my foot in it more deeply. "You are excellent. Whom
do you guide?"

"Tourists."

Miss Goto leads me down some steps at the back of the shrine
to a garden of raked sand, which we enter across some stepping
stones; facing the garden is the main building of the temple, a long,
low, sober structure with a handsome tiled roof, but its paper doors
are all shut and this gives the building a blind look; behind the
raked sand are rocks, a gnarled tree, and then shrubs and pines
above which rise one of the wooded hills of the city's eastern bound-
ary. Miss Goto goes eagerly forward and then comes to a standstill
with her back to the temple; she changes her position several times,
squinting through her glasses like a painter trying to decide where to
put the easel. At last her mind is made up and, slipping out of her
shoes she steps up on to the temple veranda.

"Here." She beckons.

"Shoes off? Must I?"

"I am sorry."

Slowly, I obey.

"Now," says Miss Goto, when I have joined her on the veranda,
"this garden is called the Crane and Turtle Garden."

"Oh?"

"Yes. You see the small tree on the left? That has been trained
to grow in the shape of a turtle, and the one on the right is a crane."

To me, both trees are dwarf pines that have been forced to grow
sideways instead of upwards—the Japanese are fond of whimsy—but I
don't disappoint Miss Goto. "Marvelous! You know Kyoto is in a way
like Rome. I had an aunt who lived in Rome. She's dead now, but—"

"Oh, I am so sorry!" Miss Goto commiserates over my aunt's death as if the fact were the point of my story. Perhaps she thinks that the beauty of the garden, which is surprisingly free of sightseers, has reminded me of my old aunt's demise.

"Her death was hardly a tragedy, Miss Goto. She was eighty-six when she died. The point I wished to make was that she used to say that although she'd lived in Rome for fifty years, she still didn't know the city completely and was always discovering something new. I feel the same about Kyoto. I have been here many times, but I have never seen the library, nor have I seen this beautiful garden."

"Thank you."

We sit on the veranda with our legs dangling down. I open my black Chinese fan, which I bought in Hong Kong, and fan Miss Goto's moist face, but she doesn't seem to like such attention for she moves away a little. Suddenly, she says, "Excuse me," takes the fan from me and begins to fan my face instead. I let her do so and think about where I shall take her to lunch, wondering whether we should go to the efficiently air-conditioned grill room of the Kyoto Hotel or to my house, where I might cook her an omelette, or perhaps she knows how to cook an omelette.

"That's enough, thank you, Miss Goto. I feel quite cool now."

She folds the fan carefully, hands it back to me, and then gazes at the garden. I examine her profile. Her features are quite good— her nose is no smaller than most Japanese noses, her teeth do not protrude, and her thickish black eyebrows suit the pallor of her face, and the pallor itself is interesting, giving her a kind of theatrical appearance, a "Noh-play" look. The general effect, though, because of the rimless glasses, the straight hair, the faded, flowered dress, is spinsterish and fails to excite; perhaps, unconsciously, it is not meant to. Physically, Miss Goto is less attractive than Noriko, but because I do not know her well she is more appealing to me than the latter, and, intellectually, she is Noriko's superior by a long chalk. In spite of her Western education, Miss Goto would be the Japanese wife *par excellence*, and, as far as I can judge from observing friends, the old-fashioned Japanese wife is the most amenable sort of spouse one could have, though Japanese husbands do not always seem to think so since they are spoiled.

I look at Miss Goto again. Her desire to immolate herself, her

exaggerated self-effacement could, surely, never turn into possessive-
ness, jealousy, petulance, or shrewishness. Being thirty-five and past
the marriageable age, she would be so thankful to find a husband
that she would never dare object, however monstrously he behaved.
Marriage with Miss Goto might not be a bad idea, I think as I look
at the turtle and then at the crane.

Miss Goto slides off the veranda into her shoes.

"It's time to go," she says.

"Where would you like to lunch?"

"I must go to my office."

"I was hoping you'd lunch with me."

"You're very kind. Another time."

21

I am not going to buy Kazumi a pearl brooch,
nor am I going to give her the bamboo one,
which is still in the drawer of my desk. Last
night and the night before I made overt
advances and was repulsed, politely, of course,
but firmly. My vanity is hurt for now I must
conclude that her reasons for staying here are the luxuries which she
does not have in her one-room apartment: the color TV set, the
shower, the air conditioner, and my cooking. A month has passed
and she is still ensconced and unmolested. The strange thing is that
I am not angry with her. I am hurt, naturally—who isn't by a
rebuff?—but I like her to be around; I look forward to her return
from work in the evening, and—this is a sure test of love—I enjoy
cooking for her. Last night I made my risotto yet again and she was
ecstatic about it, declaring it to be more excellent than ever.

Although I have even less to say to her than I do to Noriko—
for having known Noriko for a number of years we have a peopled
past to talk about and can say between silence, "D'you remember so-
and-so?"—I feel less bored, far less bored with Kazumi. I can even
watch Kazumi gape at television without having the slightest attack
of ennui. I may feel frustrated, envious of Sabu-chan, but I do not
feel bored. Perhaps I am in love. An unrequited love for someone

who is indifferent isn't a very sensible position to allow oneself to get into. It has again occurred to me that the two women may have made a kind of pact, some Japanese agreement against the foreigner, whose terms preclude any liaison between Kazumi and me, and as I suspected at the time that was what they talked about on the telephone when Noriko rang up to report her safe arrival in Tokyo. Why does Kazumi allow me to kiss her? Admittedly, the kiss is usually turned into the sort of peck one gives an aunt, for at the moment of impact she moves her head and my lips land on her cheek. The agreement may permit such chaste kissing, which is supposed to keep me from philandering any further; if so, Noriko has more wile than I credited her with, or is it that all females have a reserve of cunning?

These kisses that I now plant on Kazumi's cheek are beginning to disturb me—during the day when she is out as well as at night when she is at the top of the ladder stairs on the other side of the house. The only thing to do is to try someone else, and the only other person easily available, apart from bar hostesses, whom I abhor, is Miss Goto. I shall try her.

I spend most of the morning at my desk thinking about Miss Goto and listening to three cicadas screeching on the paulownia tree outside the south window, the bean-curd man's horn, the traffic, and the girls' band, which now moves up and down the scale quite smoothly. I wait for Misa-san to go and then I ring Miss Goto.

Immediately she says, "Thank you very much for the other day."

"Thank you for showing me such fascinating places, I loved the—"

"I am afraid it was very tedious for you."

"Not in the least."

"I apologize for taking you to such dull and uninteresting places, please—"

We go on like this, absurdly, for a few minutes (I feel it is a kind of game), and then I ask her to lunch. "At about twelve-thirty tomorrow then? Could you come to my house?"

"Thank you very much. I am sure it will be a great trouble for you."

"But no. Not in the least."

She agrees to come. Tomorrow is Saturday, a free day for her but not for Kazumi. That is why I asked her to lunch and not to dinner. I do not wish Kazumi to know about my meetings with Miss Goto because she might tell Noriko, and it's better that Noriko doesn't know about my amorous activities. I'll feel less guilty if she remains ignorant of them.

I awake as usual at dawn but a few pages of a book on Wittgenstein soon send me back to sleep and I do not stir till after nine. I hear Misa-san talking in the kitchen. Why hasn't Kazumi gone to work? I want her to be out as Miss Goto is coming to lunch today. Downstairs I hasten, to discover that Kazumi is taking the day off.

"Why?" I ask, sounding more like an uncompromising taskmaster than a would-be lover who ought to be pleased that she was going to stay at home.

"I feel a little unwell."

"Oh? I am sorry. But won't it matter not going to the office?"

"I be absent."

"I see."

"It does not matter."

Shocked, rather, and disconcerted at Kazumi's indifference towards her job, I go to the bathroom.

"Are you sure it doesn't matter being absent?" I ask when she brings my breakfast tray to me in the sitting room.

"It does not matter." Kazumi is in her brief shorts, which means, presumably, that she is not going out.

It is difficult to settle down to work upstairs because in addition to the customary extraneous noises such as the cicadas, the girls' band, the bean-curd man's horn, and the throbbing of the diesel-engined lorries, there is the inner worry about whether Kazumi is going to be in at midday. I do not want her to know that I have invited Miss Goto to lunch.

After an hour or so, Kazumi comes up to my room. "I shall cook a special lunch for you," she announces.

"I'm afraid I have to go out for lunch."

Her face falls. "Go out?"

"Yes."

"You must go out for lunch?"

"Yes." I stare at the books on the shelf in front of me.

"Who you take lunch with?"

"Mr. Watkins." I know at once that I have lied unconvincingly.

"*So?*"

"Yes." I glance at her and our eyes meet, but her glare is too penetrating; I flick my eyes away.

"Where you take lunch with Professor Watkins?"

"At the Kyoto Hotel. I am sorry. Tonight you can cook dinner."

"Tonight, I go out." She turns and descends the stairs.

 I spend the rest of the morning at my desk wondering what to do about Miss Goto. I decide that the only course is to go out just before twelve-thirty and meet her round the corner in the main street. At about a quarter to twelve the lane resounds with the garbage bell, the warning that the refuse wagon is on its way and that dustbins must be put outside the houses. I hear Misa-san and Kazumi below carrying through the house the plastic dustbin and the hefty wooden box in which we put our dry rubbish. Will the dustmen come before or after twelve-thirty? If they come after that hour I will have nothing to worry about, but if they come before and Miss Goto is early then Kazumi may see her because she will go into the lane to take in the dustbin and the box as Misa-san goes home at noon. By twelve-thirty the dustmen have not arrived, so I decide to leave the house and wait around the corner in the shade of the roofed temple gate.

"I'm going now, then, Kazumi-san," I call. She is looking at television. "Please don't forget the dustbins."

She gets up and switches off the television set.

"I didn't mean to disturb you."

She stands on the *genkan* step while I put on my shoes.

"Where you go?" she asks.

"Just out to lunch."

"Professor Watkins's house?"

"We're meeting in town." I slide open the front door. "See you later."

I begin to push the door to but at that moment the garbage bell rings again and into the lane comes the refuse wagon for which there is only just enough room. I have to wait on the doorstep until the truck has passed to squeeze by. It is not possible. Kazumi joins me on the step. The wagon passes and stops, revealing behind it a posse of virile dustmen with white kerchiefs round their heads in the manner of samurai about to fight, and Miss Goto wearing a kimono and holding an open parasol. The dustmen, grunting and shouting, energetically seize the dustbins and empty them into the truck's gaping cavity—the quick, deft movements of the men, the flowered kimono, and the parasol flash me back for a moment if not into Japan's past then right into a samurai film: here is an acrobatic fight, a great show of virility watched by an elegant lady.

While the agile men are whirling into the air the dustbins from the house opposite, I break out of my spell and hasten towards Miss Goto.

"The dustmen are here. Do you mind lunching out?" I go on, not daring to look round, the back of my head stinging as if a powerful ray had been turned on to it. The effects of the ray lessen when I have gone round the corner. I wait by the temple gate for Miss Goto, who is waddling after me ducklike in her wedged *zori*. Will Kazumi follow? Did she notice Miss Goto? Or did the dustmen occupy her attention as they did mine at first? Did Miss Goto see Kazumi or was her view screened by her parasol?

"It's too hot to stand about here," I say to the bewildered Miss Goto. "Let's take a taxi." I advance to the corner of the two main roads. "Which would you prefer: the grill room of the Kyoto Hotel or a Japanese restaurant?"

"Just as you wish, Mr. Meadowes."

A bus is coming and going in the right direction.

"Let's take the bus."

By luck the traffic lights change, stopping the bus and allowing us to cross. Like an obedient Japanese wife, Miss Goto hurries after me. In the role of Japanese husband, I board the bus first, leaving Miss Goto to clamber up the high steps in her awkward *zori*, which have slipped sideways to resemble weights; hobbled she is, in her

Japanese sandals. The lights turn green, the bus lurches forward. Through the window I can see Kazumi coming out of our lane and crossing the street. Is she looking for me or has she merely gone out to buy some Japanese food? When she is alone, she usually eats noodles, which she prefers, I suspect, to Western food, in spite of her exclamations of "*Oishii!*" at my dishes.

I suspect too that Miss Goto would rather have Japanese food than a Western-style menu in the grill room of the Kyoto Hotel, but of course she agrees that we should go to the hotel.

We sit facing each other at a table for four. A waiter gives us each an outrageously large menu which embarrasses Miss Goto and for some reason me. The list of dishes seems so ostentatious, so out of keeping with the delicate taste of the country, a reminder of the vulgarity of the West.

"What would you like to have, Miss Goto?"

She shuts her menu. "Please choose."

"What would you like, though?" To me half the fun of eating out is discussing what one will have, deciding, changing one's mind after the waiter has noted the order, and then fixing on something different. Miss Goto is like Noriko, who, in the hundreds of meals I have had in her company, has never once chosen a dish for herself, nearly always having the same as I, even though she may not much care for it. Miss Goto's lack of initiative disappoints me, but since she is in my good books I am indulgent and suggest to her some items on the menu. I choose *paté maison* with toast and grilled trout to follow. Miss Goto will not drink, so I order half a bottle of white wine for myself.

"How are you getting along in Kyoto, Mr. Meadowes?"

"Very well, really, but it is hot, isn't it?" An idea suddenly comes to me. "The air conditioner has broken down in my house and the place has been like a Turkish bath."

"I am sorry."

"That is why I thought it better that we should lunch out."

"You have no electric fan?"

"Yes, but I find—"

"In my house we do not have an electric fan."

Conversation does not rattle along as I had thought it might when I had daydreamed at the barber's about a meal with Miss Goto in the very same grill room where we are now sitting; it becomes labored; as soon as I have made one remark I have to prepare a fresh one in my mind. Miss Goto never introduces a subject. We race through many topics—Shakespeare (she likes *Hamlet*, but she has never seen a live performance of the play, nor has she seen the Russian film, or even the Olivier version); a recent art exhibition (she did not see it); modern British poets (she says "Yes" to all my views) —and exhaust them at once. She is much less communicative than she was at tea in my house. Is she shy because she is in a "smart" Western-style restaurant, or is it that being in a kimono she feels she should be the demure Japanese maiden? I take refuge in the weather and I talk of the heat, although it is cool in the air-conditioned grill room, but the heat becomes the only thing we seem to be able to discuss with ease, and we return to it as a learner driver returns to the driveway of his house: with relief. If Noriko were with me and not Miss Goto we should have sat in comparatively comfortable silence. I know Noriko well enough for a glum silence not to matter, but with an acquaintance such as Miss Goto a moment without words is painful.

"What would you like to see this afternoon, Mr. Meadowes?"

"I don't know." My plan had been to flirt with Miss Goto, but Kazumi's presence disallows a return to the house. "It's so hot. I wish my air conditioner wasn't out of order."

"How about Chishakuin temple?"

"Is it far?"

"Opposite the museum. You haven't seen it?"

"No, but isn't it rather hot for temple viewing?"

"There are some famous screens."

"All right."

The fact that Miss Goto wants to show me the temple is encouraging; on the other hand she might feel obliged to do something in return for the lunch. While I am paying the bill at the cashier's desk, Miss Goto trots off to the Ladies' in an anxious, hurried walk. As I am descending the open stairway to the busy lobby, where arriving and departing American package-tour groups are assembling, I stop and gasp, for threading his way through the tourists and their baggage from the reception desk to the lifts is Bob. Just as I am about to call out, he emerges from the cluster of gray-

and-blue-haired ladies, joining a Japanese girl and disappearing into
the elevator with her before I have time to do a double-take. The
girl is Kazumi. Presumably he is taking her up to the dining room,
but how was the date so quickly arranged?

23

"Are you feeling all right, Mr. Meadowes?"

"Yes," I answer, untruthfully. "I think it
must have been the fish."

It is the second time that Miss Goto has
asked me this question as we travel across the
city to the wretched temple which she wants
me to see. I must look *distrait* or worried and the Japanese are extra-
ordinarily quick to sense one's mood. I am worried, in a way. Is
Kazumi deceiving me? Obviously, she made a plan. Has she really
fallen for Bob or is she just using his philanderer's nature to taunt
me? By the time our taxi has turned out of Kawaramachi into Shijo
Street I have assumed the latter contingency. Kazumi is with Bob in
order to make me jealous. I told her I was lunching with him at the
Kyoto Hotel and she guessed, rightly, that I was lunching there and
went there with Bob to confront me. She must be furious that she
missed me. Did she see Miss Goto? We turn right at the Yasaka
Shrine and join the line of snorting, stinking trucks going south
along Higashiyama-dori.

We leave the taxi at the foot of the steps outside the temple.
The sun beats down on my bare head and Miss Goto puts up her
parasol and holds it over me. If Kazumi has fallen for Bob, why
didn't she do so before? Or is she one of his regulars?

A priest in white kimono tears our entrance tickets in two after
we have taken off our shoes, and then an old man with a scraggly,
gray beard and a stick, dressed only in long cotton underpants and a
vest, takes charge of us. Miss Goto mumbles about the temple into
my ear, but the old man wishes to show he still has some use in the
world and, taking hold of my shirt sleeve, tugs me along the pol-
ished boards of the veranda, off which are matted rooms with painted sliding doors. We stop at the first room.

"The Cherry Blossom Room," he says, pointing to the shoji, "Painted by Hasegawa Tohaku for Hideyoshi in 1592."

"The temple is almost a complete renovation," explains Miss Goto, who is on my other side.

"Very old," says the old man.

"Due to a fire," says Miss Goto.

The voices of the old man and Miss Goto are like those unwanted and unrequested tunes that are boomed into one's ears in cafes, bars, and hotels, and so I do not pay much attention to what my two guides are saying. The heat and Kazumi have sent me into a daze.

"Founded by Ieyasu, the first Tokugawa shogun . . ." The old man is determined to impart his knowledge.

What about Bob's wife? Can she be so much the Japanese spouse, so *casanière* that she never knows what her husband is doing?

"This temple was originally in the Kii Peninsula . . ."

"Burnt down." The ominous words come from Miss Goto and sound peculiarly oracular.

Bob must be the sort of man who covets other people's possessions or lovers, though Kazumi has been neither possessed nor loved by me.

The old man waves a bony, veined hand at the garden. "Designed by Sen no Rikyu, tea master in the Momoyama Period."

Just as the Japanese must return a kindness with neurotic punctiliousness, so they will get their own back in the end. Is Kazumi doing that? Is she having a sort of revenge because she saw me meet Miss Goto in the lane? She then rang Bob to test if I had been lying, and discovering I had been she persuaded Bob to take her to the Kyoto Hotel so as to have a confrontation with me, and Bob agreed to her request because she is more than a friend and therefore can make him do things for her.

We mount two high steps into the main hall of the temple, open on three sides to the garden; the fourth side is occupied by the altar, a mass of gold ornaments and caskets giving a cluttered, muddled effect; in the gloom at the back stands a dark wooden statue of the Buddha, whose features are impossible to distinguish.

The old man says, "This is the headquarters of the Chizan

school of the Shingon sect, one of the largest Buddhist sects in Japan."

"But divided, divided into nine branches."

"Kobo-Daishi was the founder of this sect."

"He lived in the ninth century."

Noriko belongs to the Nichiren sect of Buddhism, the biggest according to guidebook figures. I have never known her to show the slightest interest in her religion. She will throw a ten-yen coin into the large wooden box in front of the altar, clap her hands, and mutter a prayer, but I think that doing this amounts to no more than performing an act of superstition. I don't think she believes at all, and goes through such a ritual simply because it might bring her luck.

I once asked her what her prayer was about. "I pray for you," she replied, self-righteously. I felt stifled. It was at a little fishing village in Chiba Prefecture called Kominato. We had gone there from our hotel in Tateyama on Tokyo Bay after having a row. She had become all sentimental at about six in the morning and had awakened me by clinging to me passionately as if she were drowning. I broke free and said, "Don't be such a bore! I want to sleep." Whereupon Noriko jumped up, dressed, and ran out of the room. I tried to fall asleep again but visions of Noriko walking into the sea disturbed me. I got up and hastened to the beach. Far off there was a speck of a person walking by the edge of the water. I followed, and the speck stopped, enabling me to catch it up. It was Noriko, of course. She had stopped because a stream flowed into the sea at this point and she could go no farther.

"I am sorry, Noriko."

She looked at me and then walked away towards the river mouth. I followed. She then made a sudden impulsive movement, and in a few seconds was wading into the water but the water was shallow and only came up to her chubby calves. I laughed. "You can't drown yourself there. There's not enough water."

She turned. Her face was puckered with worry and indecision, then her expression changed and she laughed too. The crisis was over, but Noriko took advantage of my having behaved badly. "Please hold me," she simpered, "it is stony." I went into the water and assisted her out with an arm round her waist, and then escorted her to the hotel, where in order to put things right I made love to her.

The old man in the temple is muttering, "I used to be an electrical engineer. Now I have retired and I live in this temple." He goes on to talk about the university in Tokyo where he was once a student.

"Mr. Meadowes teaches English at that university."

"*Aa so desu ka?*" The old man's eyes show not a sparkle of interest; when he finds a listener, the old man only wants to talk of himself. I am not a listener because Kazumi has all my attention, but Miss Goto lends a sympathetic ear to the old man's outpourings about his life, his recent retirement to this temple.

I stand in the torrid temple oblivious to everything except the sweat that trickles down my body from my armpits and my throat and to Kazumi. I try to remember the incidents of the last few weeks. What have I done wrong?

With Noriko the sexual act has never been entirely satisfactory— is this why I am unable to recall any golden episodes? That same act, which can be both futile and rapturous, has never been satisfactory with my wife either, but there have been moments of ecstasy with her. Such moments occurred when our minds communed: at Baalbek, which we both saw for the first time together; once when we were slightly tipsy on *raki* at noon in a cafe in the Taurus mountains; and again when we stole a swim (Monica is an excellent swimmer) in the sea near Kavalla on our way from Salonika to Istanbul. There are many golden episodes I can recall with my wife.

Can I recall any such moments with anyone else? No, not really. I suppose there were a few whores who gave me pleasure or relief, but I don't remember any of them with delight. I suppose it is my fate to remain sexually unsatisfied.

Noriko has never excited me. Why, then, have I continued to know her? I have always told myself that Noriko deserved to be rewarded for her loyalty, and it would be unfair to give her up; therefore, out of an absurd sense of duty, a sense of fair play instilled in me from birth, I have continued to see her. This is what I have told myself and I have given myself several medals for my steadfast "service." Is this true? Is it only out of a fear of the consequences that I refrain from breaking with her? My mind then turns to Kazumi, who for some unknown reason attracts me enormously. I can't help thinking of her most of the time. I have become obsessed, which is a silly morbid state to be in, but I can do nothing about it. I realize that I am jealous of Bob. He's turned out to be a dark horse, a snake in the grass.

I break out of my sweaty reverie to find that my companions have gone. I search about the shining wooden passages and find Miss Goto and the old man in one of the matted rooms sitting on the floor and drinking green tea by a table on which there is an electric fan.

"I've been looking for you all over the place," I say, a little ill-humoredly.

"You seemed so far away in your thoughts. I didn't like to disturb you."

"Won't you have some tea?" asks the old man.

"Yes, please."

The old man pours out a cup of yellow-green liquid and passes it across the table. I lower myself onto a cushion, and, then, the old man heaves himself to his feet with the aid of his stick and a cry of "*Oisho!*" and pads off down the passage.

"Perhaps it is time to go home," Miss Goto suggests.

"I can't rest in my house," I reply. "It's too hot there. It's cooler here under this fan than it is in my little hot box. Have you any ideas?" I push my foot against her leg, which is folded underneath her, as, typically, she is sitting on her heels in polite fashion. She gives me a coy glance; she has taken off her glasses so I'm not sure how clearly she can see me. I keep my foot pressed to her leg. "What about the cinema? Would you like to go to see a film? The cinemas are air-conditioned."

"So are the pachinko parlors," she retorts with surprising sarcasm.

"Yes, but it's not a game for me. The balls make ones's hands so dirty."

"Do you play often?"

"I've played once. That was enough." An idea comes to me. "I should like a bath, a Japanese bath. The way to become cool is to get really hot first, and then to lie under a fan in a *yukata*. Would you like a bath?"

Miss Goto looks down.

"Would you?"

"There is a public bathhouse near my house."

"I don't want to go to a public bathhouse. Let us go to a small hotel and have a bath." I decide that I should try and forget Kazumi for the moment and make the best of the company I have chosen for the afternoon.

Miss Goto does not answer. I imagine it is the first time that such a proposition has been made to her. The terrific heat has the effect of emboldening me as if I had a fever. I persist. "What do you think of my idea?"

"Perhaps I should go home."

"It's too early to go home." I lean towards her and say in what I hope is a seductive voice, "What would you like to do this afternoon, Miss Goto?"

"I'll leave it to you."

I take this to mean that she wants to accompany me to a hotel.

24 During my affair with Noriko, I sometimes met a bar hostess called Akiko. I think of Akiko now during the taxi ride with Miss Goto from the temple to the *hôtels de passe* quarter, a distance of little more than a mile, and I realize I do so because the few times I took Akiko out of her bar (How long I had to wait until she was free! The delay was a device of the mama-san to keep me drinking and buying phony drinks for the hostess) we went to one of the "love" hotels or *abekku* (from the French *avec*) hotels as the Japanese, who are fond of euphemisms, call such establishments. The sessions with Akiko were never satisfactory because whores and sordid bedrooms act as an anaphrodisiac upon me. I find myself wondering about the last man my partner was with, what the hotel proprietor thinks, and my speculations put me off and all I want to do is get it over with and return to my own bed.

Now I am leading Miss Goto towards the very sort of place that I went to with Akiko and which I found abhorrent; it is possible to do so because it is a new experience, because Miss Goto isn't a whore, and because the Kyoto *abekku* hotels are charming provided one doesn't visit them too often. I have only been to this quarter of the ancient capital two or three times before and each time to a different hotel with a different bargirl.

Out of discretion, I let the taxi pass the *torii* of the shrine by the lane that leads to this notorious district, and after we have gone two hundred yards I tell the driver to stop. I get out, but Miss Goto stays in the taxi.

"Come along," I coax.

"We get out here?"

"Yes."

"You want to visit that shrine? It is nothing. It is—"

"Never mind. I want to visit it."

Does she really think that? Had she not meant that she was willing to have a bath with me?

We walk back to the shrine and when instead of going through the *torii* I lead her past it to the head of the lane, she stops.

"I cannot."

"Please."

"I have never been to such a place before."

"Time to begin."

I start down the lane on one side of which is the drive to the shrine buildings that is used as a car park, and on the other little two-story, terraced, wooden houses all with signs showing the prices of rooms "for a rest" and for all night. Miss Goto makes heavy weather of the uneven lane and hobbles after me, her *zori* catching in the cracks in the asphalt. At the bottom of the slope the lane joins another which has similar miniature hotels in it; so fragile do they seem that I feel that if I lost my temper and struck out I could demolish the whole quarter. I look around. Miss Goto, chin on chest, is regarding the ground and shuffling one sandal ahead of the other as if she were negotiating a minefield.

"Come along."

"Mr. Meadowes . . . this . . . district . . . I . . . I cannot . . ."

Just round the corner is a hotel whose door is open. I go back to Miss Goto, grasp her wrist, and pull her into the dark *genkan* of the hotel. She keeps her head down.

A demure woman in a neat, dark kimono kneels on the *genkan* step and welcomes us, and then with an automatic movement produces two pairs of slippers from a cupboard at her side. For the amount of surprise she shows, Miss Goto and I might have been staying at the hotel for the past week.

Miss Goto hesitates.

"Come along." My tone is quite schoolmasterish. I slip off my shoes and step into the hotel and then fluttering her wide sleeves and fussing over her *zori*—putting them tidily together on the step—Miss Goto follows me and the hotel manageress up a steep flight of narrow stairs to a small Japanese room on the floor of which are already laid a futon and two little pillows. The manageress switches on a fan and leaves the room, carefully sliding the door to. Miss Goto and I sit opposite each other on the floor with a low table between us.

"We must wait for the tea," I warn. I know the drill.

Miss Goto buries her chin in her neck so that I can only see the top of her head.

Silence.

There is a discreet tap on the door and in reply to my "*Dozo*" a comely little maid in a white blouse and a navy blue skirt (she reminds me of the schoolgirls opposite my house) brings in two cups of green tea, two boiled sweets, and two folded *yukata*. I ask if we may have a bath. We may, if we don't mind waiting for about ten minutes as the bathroom is occupied. The maid is younger, more attractive, and physically more desirable than my friend. While kneeling in the passage in order to slide the door to, she gives me a lascivious look.

When she has gone, I rise and fasten the little catch on the door. I take off my sweat-soaked shirt and my trousers and put on one of the identically patterned *yukata*. Miss Goto does not act the Japanese wife and take my clothes from me; she keeps her face hidden like a devout spinster friend of my mother's who used so to kneel in church.

"Won't you have some tea, Miss Goto?"

"No, thank you."

"What's the matter?"

"Nothing."

"We'll be able to have a bath soon."

No reply.

"Wouldn't you like that, Miss Goto? We'll be able to have a bath together."

No reply.

I stare at the top of Miss Goto's head for a while and then I crawl round the table and look up at her face. She is crying. "Oh God!" I exclaim. "Really, Miss Goto, what is wrong in coming to a hotel for a rest on a hot afternoon? Perfectly natural, I call it."

"It is the first time."

"There has to be a first time for everything, you know."

"That girl was so terrible."

"She didn't seem so to me." I am surprised that Miss Goto noticed her.

"She was horrible." Miss Goto sniffs, dabs her eyes with a handkerchief which she takes from the fold in her kimono. "How am I going to get out of here?"

"By the door," I say facetiously.

She is too distraught to laugh.

"People may see me."

"Who?"

"Friends."

"Is it likely that any of your friends would be marching up and down this quarter on a sweltering afternoon in August?"

"They might be."

"Then we can wait till after dark before leaving. I'm going to have a bath, are you?"

"No, thank you."

"What will you do then?"

"I'll wait here, Mr. Meadowes, I suppose." She sighs. "Oh, Mr. Meadowes, I do wish you had not brought me to this place! I feel, er, I cannot describe how I feel. I feel like Clarissa."

I laugh. Miss Goto remains serious; hurt, too, she seems, by my hilarity; probably she does really feel like the unfortunate Clarissa.

"Are you sure you don't want a bath, Miss Goto?"

She looks at me pleadingly. "Mr. Meadowes, this is the first time I have been in a hotel bedroom alone with a man and I feel—"

"You've just said you feel like Clarissa. All I can say is there's not the remotest need for you to be afraid. I am not Lovelace. I shall go and have a bath."

25

The small cypress wood bath is half empty. I turn on the taps, sit on the little wooden stool, and forlornly wash myself. Noriko used to soap my back and I would soap hers, we would sit in the tub together with water spilling over the side; it was deliciously voluptuous.

When I get upstairs again, I find that Miss Goto has gone.

I lie on the futon in the bedroom with the fan turned on my damp body. The Japanese manage to wash and dry themselves with the same postage-stamp towel, but I have never been able to do this, especially not on a steamy afternoon when as fast as one mops up the water on one's body it is replaced by sweat.

For some unfathomable reason I think of the time when Noriko became pregnant. It was not long after she had guessed that I knew a bargirl; in a moment of exasperation I had mentioned the name of a bar—"You know a girl there, don't you?" Noriko said over and over again until I said, "Yes. Her name is Chiaki." Noriko threatened to have the child in spite of the fact that in Japan abortion is legal and not very expensive. I was furious with her for she had promised me that matters had been looked after and that there was no danger of her becoming pregnant. "I want to have your child. I want to keep it," she said, repeatedly, as if she were talking of a souvenir. From the first, I suspect that she had failed to take precautions on purpose. Oh, the hell I went through! The advantage she took of her condition! She became smug, demanding, self-righteous, accusatory. Finally, just before the end of the best time for the operation, she agreed to have it, though not until love-me-forever promises had been wrung out of me. What else could I have done but acquiesce? The financial cost was nugatory; the cost in emotional strain, however, was high and the upshot of the whole sordid business was that I ended up almost hating Noriko for a while.

It was never very hard to put Noriko off, though. Fundamentally she is sweet-natured and therefore easy to deceive. I sometimes invented an academic party or the visit of a friend of my wife who might report home, and these excuses were accepted without too much demur, but when I met a new "mistress" I would feel guilty and have visions of Noriko's seeing us by chance. In spite of the vastness of Tokyo and the unlikelihood of a fortuitous encounter, I would be ill at ease in a restaurant, a theater or a cinema; not until I was in an *abekku* hotel did I feel safe from discovery, and then once in the hotel I longed to leave it.

I put on my *yukata* and slide open the door of my "short-time" bedroom—how absurd to be in such a place alone! Through the paper door of the room opposite issue grunts and while descending the stair as cautiously as an old age pensioner, I hear little coos, unrestrained and ecstatic. I decide to go in search of the maid who brought the tea.

The manageress (she must realize my frustration as Miss Goto has gone; it's impossible to leave a Japanese inn secretly, as one must get one's shoes) gives me an orange juice in what I suppose is her bed-sitting-room–storeroom–office, a tatami room with a television set and a guitar in the alcove, and, in a corner, a crate of beer and another of Coca-Cola; festooned round the walls are clothes (both male and female ones) on hangers, and in another corner is a pile of folded *yukata*.

"Your friend gone."

"She was frightened. Pity."

"You like massage?" The manageress jerks her head at the door.

"Yes. No."

She inclines her head, rises to her feet, goes out of the room.

There is a noise of shuffling slippers in the passage. A voice says, "*Gomen nasai.*" Then follows the sound of voices and the tinkling of a little bell.

A man's voice says, "*Arigato gozaimashita.*"

From the manageress comes, "*Domo sumimasen.*"

A third voice, Japanese, female and squeaky, says, "*Mata dozo.*"

More tinkles, the scraping of shoes, grunts, the shutting of a door, and then the maid who served the tea enters. Her face is rosy, smiling, and round; it is a country face. She has changed from her blouse and skirt into one of the hotel's *yukata*. Unshyly, she kneels in front of me; carefully, she tucks her robe under her and then spreads her dainty hands on her thighs. My eyes trace a line from her sensual, parted lips, down her slender throat to the gap in her *yukata*, which discloses the tops of her breasts; they rest there for a moment, and then travel up the same route to meet her eyes, which are expectant and lustful.

She puts a hand on my knee.

"Massage?" she says.

"No, thanks." I decide that I don't want her. I don't want whorish, pretense love. I want Kazumi. I go up to my room to dress.

26

"*Sumimasen*," I say in my English accent.

The manageress picks up a long shoehorn to the end of which is attached a little bell, a device to deter clients from departing without notice.

The bell tinkles as I use it to ease on my shoes and again when I return it to the manageress's little hand.

"Please come again," says the maid. The blue and white *yukata* is now closed modestly; there are no gaps. She gives no sign of annoyance at my rejecting her.

"*Mata dozo*," mumbles the manageress. And she and the masseuse incline their heads towards me in a graceful gesture of respect.

Although it is dusk, I go hastily out of the hotel and walk up the lane at the pace of a respectable commuter (I think of Miss Goto and wonder in what sort of order she made her retreat) to the main road, where I hail a passing taxi. Will Miss Goto ever forgive me? Will she tell her mother that I tried to seduce her? And Kazumi—is she with Bob?

Stuck in my front door as a sort of reproach is an air-letter from my wife, which bears an American stamp and a San Francisco postmark. She is approaching. Damn! I do not wish to be reminded of her at this particular moment so I put the letter unopened on the chest in the *genkan*. Kazumi, of course, is not in. Is she in an *abekku* hotel with Bob? I pour out a large whiskey, gulp it down, and then go to the *genkan* to get Monica's letter. She is staying with the Crawfords in their "beautiful house" and will fly to Tokyo, after a week in Hawaii, towards the end of the month. I pour out another large whiskey, turn on the television set, and lower myself onto the tatami. To save struggling to my feet, I crawl into the dining recess and ring Bob. His wife tells me that he is out. I lean against the bench seat and fitfully watch a singing contest for amateurs. Teenagers (of both sexes one presumes, although their sex is not easy to specify) bawl "pop" numbers into a microphone which is shaped like a big succulent lollipop and is almost indecently suggestive; as they sing, the singers make stiff, stagy gestures with their hands. How tired one gets of certain tunes! I get up, pour out a third and even larger whiskey, open a packet of peanuts, and return to the bench seat. I devour the nuts with a voracity which makes me realize that I am hungry. What about dinner? The Kyoto Hotel, of course. Perhaps Bob and Kazumi will be there; maybe they checked in and took a room. I shall go there and dine.

No one in the name of Watkins is staying in the hotel. It seems ironical that the only vacant table is the one I shared with Miss Goto at lunch, and feeling devil-may-care I sit in the chair that she occupied. While perusing the menu, which is not good enough to read twice in the same day, I order a double whiskey, and then, unadventurously, I choose a steak. Can it really be true that Kazumi is still with Bob? Perhaps she finds him attractive; although he is older than I, he knows Japanese and Japanese ways far better than I, and anyway the father type is often admired here and Bob is decidedly more fatherly than I. By the time I have finished my steak, I realize that I am jealous of Bob, jealous of someone whom I had always taken to be rather an ass. I pay my bill, leave the hotel, and walk aimlessly down Kawaramachi.

27

It is Sunday morning. I have a hangover and I am on the floor in the sitting room. When I left the Kyoto Hotel last evening, I walked down Kawaramachi and ran into Professor Nakayama, whom I had met before somewhere. He insisted on taking me to a bar. He had just been to a British Council party and was flushed and loquacious. He talked on and on about Alice Meynell, claiming, as far as I can remember, that she was Britain's greatest poet. The whiskey, the professor, and Alice Meynell, the thought of my wife's impending arrival, and, subsequently, a bargirl drove Kazumi out of the forefront of my mind for an hour or two, but she came back into my consciousness strongly enough for me to fend off the bargirl's advances and the professor's encouraging me to take the baggage to a hotel.

The telephone rings and my "hello" receives a faint, tremulous reply, "I am very sorry." My heart flutters and my blood pressure rises out of nervousness and shame; it is Miss Goto. I say nothing for a few seconds and she repeats, "I am very sorry, Mr. Meadowes, for my bad behavior last night, I mean yesterday afternoon."

"It is I who should apologize, Miss Goto. I was carried away. It must have been the heat."

"No, no, my behavior requires an explanation, but not on the telephone."

"Quite."

"On Wednesday is our O-Bon Festival. Do you know about O-Bon, Mr. Meadowes?"

"Yes."

"Well then, I was thinking that you might like to see the Daimonji Festival when the hills around Kyoto are lighted with fires that form many different shapes." She takes a breath and then goes on timidly in travelese, "For example, the character *dai*, meaning "big," is lit on one hill and the character *hon*, meaning "law," is lit on another and there is . . ."

"I am afraid—"

"There are altogether five bonfires and—"

"Yes, Miss Goto, but I am afraid that on Wednesday I am not free. I have to—"

"Oh!" She sounds very disappointed.

"I'm sorry, but on Wednesday I simply can't."

"I see," she says, in a tone of gloomy resignation.

Her despair makes me relent and I ask her to dinner in the house this evening. She accepts readily.

For dinner I decide to give Miss Goto cold ham and salad, followed by fresh peaches. I know she will not complain. I wonder whether she would if she were married to me, but then she would do the catering and I the complaining. Noriko doesn't often complain, but she is capable of turning up her nose and saying, "Ma, ma," which means "so-so." Kazumi has been very polite about the meals I've cooked for her, especially about my risotto, which she seems to like very much; it's only after eating when she is lying on the bench and gazing at TV that her manners have shown room for improvement. What shall I do if she returns this evening? Nothing. Let her see Miss Goto! I saw her balding friend with the gapped teeth.

It is after midday when I go out to the shops and it is exceedingly hot. The school is not belching brass-band music, so the girls must be having their lunch break; they even practice on Sundays, but Sunday in Japan is nothing like Sunday in England. I see two brown-limbed, stalwart girls buying ice cream; they are sweet with their glistening hair in "mop" style, their white blouses and navy-blue skirts, and they look so healthy.

One of my shopping difficulties is that the aged and courteous greengrocer, the nearest one, does not always have the best vegetables, but the old man and his wife are so polite that I hate to pass them carrying paper bags from other shops. I try to remember not to buy one item on my list so that on my way home I can get it from the old man. When I pass him on my way out he bows respectfully, and if I pause to glance at his tomatoes he does not come forward and try to push them on me; he waits until I speak. In the busiest greengrocer's run by a fat man with many girl assistants, no sooner has one looked at a melon or a mound of potatoes than a girl opens a paper bag and says, "This one?" or "How many?"

I reach the old man's shop. He bows. I bow and go on making a mental note to buy a cabbage and some apples from him on my return journey. I go into the "drink" shop, which I enjoy visiting because the owner's daughter-in-law is pretty and she is usually behind the counter. She has splendid teeth and a jolly smile, but, invariably, she calls her husband, a man of about thirty who wears a peaked khaki cap, a white T-shirt, and jeans, to serve me; perhaps she feels that she cannot cope with a foreigner, although my order— beer, Coca-Cola, whiskey, orange juice—is generally the same. The girl always turns the electric fan in my direction and, while her husband is totting up the bill on the abacus, she, after he has told her to, never before, gives me a soft drink of some kind. As a rule, I order a fair amount of drink, and this never fails to surprise them. "You drink a great deal," the man says. I think he says this spontaneously because genuinely he is astonished at the amount of whiskey and beer my guests and I consume; my consumption (which is not really very great) is probably far more than that of the average Japanese household, whose menfolk have the habit of drinking in bars rather than at home. I do not think that the drink-shop man means to be censorious, for he makes his living by selling alcohol and it is to his advantage that I drink "a great deal"; nonetheless I leave the shop and walk towards the market on the other side of Sanjo Street feeling resentful at the rebuke I have been given. I don't like to be told that I drink a great deal, even though it may be true. Intrusive remarks of this kind put me off Japan.

28 In order to make the austere little sitting room less grim I bought some white chrysanthemums, and while I am arranging them the "drink man" arrives with my order. He also brings a present of six tumblers with the Suntory crest stamped on them in green. He pushes the box containing the glasses forward across the *genkan* step.

"*Dozo*," he says.

"For me?"

"*Sabisu*," he replies, meaning "service"—free, it is a present.

"Thank you very much."

Although the glasses have cost him nothing, it is kind of him to bring them. I wonder if he has done so as a softener, because he sensed this morning that I was not pleased with his remark about my drinking. At the door he bows very low and says "*Maido okini*" three times. Where else but in Japan would such a little scene occur? And it is played with such exquisite courtesy by the white-vested, khaki-capped tradesman. I return to my flower arranging feeling pro-Japanese. In the middle of my attempt to group the five chrysanthemums in the three-tiered, heaven-man-earth style that I only partly understand, Miss Goto arrives, half an hour early.

She looks down. "I am sorry."

"Why?" I decide to be in an avuncular mood and to make no reference to our meeting yesterday. "Now, Miss Goto, please come into the cool."

"Thank you."

She is wearing her faded, flowered dress, the one she wore on her first visit. She slips out of her shoes keeping her head down, and she advances into the sitting room with her chin on her chest.

"I've been trying to arrange flowers," I say, as she seems to be squinting through her rimless glasses at the low table in the corner on which stand the vase of chrysanthemums.

"I see," she mutters softly.

"Do sit down."

She sits on the edge of one of the bench seats with her back to the evening glow. I have not yet turned on the light, so it is quite dark in the room that is never bright, not even at midday.

"Would you like a drink?" I ask.

"Yes, please," she replies with surprising eagerness.

"A soft drink? I have—"

"No, thank you."

"D'you mean you'd like something alcoholic?"

"Yes, please."

"I thought you didn't drink alcohol."

"I should like to today." She still looks down as she plucks at a cushion.

"What would you like to have, then?"

"The same as you."

"A whiskey?"

"Yes, a whiskey."

"With some water and ice?"

"Just ice, please. On the rocks."

"On the rocks?" It astonishes me that Miss Goto knows the term.

"Please."

"Are you sure?"

"Yes."

"All right." I shrug and go into the kitchen, where I pour out two whiskeys, both equally strong and both only with ice. I think I may as well keep Miss Goto company and have mine "on the rocks" too; perhaps she is a secret drinker and is accustomed to alcohol, but this is so improbable. I return to the sitting room and after handing Miss Goto her whiskey I switch on the light. She holds her glass cupped in her hands swilling the whiskey round the lumps of ice and staring at them.

I raise my glass. "Cheerio!" She doesn't look up. "What's the matter, Miss Goto? Are you feeling all right?"

"It's hot," she mutters.

"It's not too bad in here, is it? The air conditioner's on. I sometimes find it too cool." I laugh feebly. "Here's to you, Miss Goto." I sip my drink. She doesn't budge. "You ought to reciprocate and drink my health as I've drunk yours," I say, as if instructing a student in Western manners.

"I'm sorry, Mr. Meadowes."

Then for the first time she looks at me. I realize at once why she has not done this before; her face is plastered with make-up unskillfully applied and she was too shy to reveal this unusual departure from modesty. "To your good health, Mr. Meadowes." She gulps her whiskey and at once begins to splutter and cough; after a few moments she recovers with an effort and gives a wan smile.

"Do you often drink whiskey?"

"Oh yes." She takes another gulp, chokes again, and dabs her eyes with a folded handkerchief.

"Perhaps you'd like some water with it. It is rather strong."

"Oh no thank you. It is very delicious."

The make-up on her usually pale, solemn face has the same effect as a Christmas-cracker mask; it mocks her, makes her clownish. Her straight black hair hangs over her cheeks and turns upwards at the end in two impertinent curls which on another face might have looked enticing, but on poor Miss Goto's they seem only to add to her grotesque appearance.

Suddenly, Miss Goto says, "May I see the house?"

Thinking that she wants to go to the lavatory, I hastily open the sitting room door and that of the bathroom. "*Dozo!*"

She peers into the bathroom. He face has taken on a high color and is embarrassing to look at.

"I see. And there are other rooms?"

"Er, yes . . ." I lead her down the dark passage to the moon-viewing room.

"You sleep here?"

"No, in another room."

I grapple with the heavy sliding windows and manage to open them halfway. "This is a very pretty room, but it is too hot."

She looks across the garden at the main house. "Is that occupied?" she asks.

"The owner is away. There is a caretaker but her quarters are on the other side of the house. I never see her."

Miss Goto's blushes clash with her rouge, making her face a bizarre study in two shades of red, not unlike the vivid make-up of a Chinese acrobat.

"There is a room above?" She glances at the ceiling. She is being as brave about her drink flush as someone with a disfiguring scar.

I do not want her to see Kazumi's things. "Yes, but my bedroom is on the other side of the house. It is also where I work."

She follows me down the dark passage, across the sitting room, and up the steep stairs to my bedroom.

I turn on the desk light. "This is the best room in the house," I say in the manner of an agent talking to a prospective tenant. "It has two views. I don't find it too hot at night." I go over to the bed-side table to switch on the fan but the plug has come out of its socket and I have to kneel on the floor to put it in. "This fan," I say, while fumbling with the plug, "has an automatic switch which you set at the hour you want it to stop and the thing turns itself off. Isn't it clever?"

The light goes out.

"Blast!" I say, still searching for the socket. "Have the lights failed?" I find the socket and insert the plug. The fan whirls into action. "They haven't, then." I get off the floor. "Why!" I give a start for Miss Goto is standing quite near and is completely nude. Her white body glows in the dark like a luminous clock.

"Miss Goto!" I recognize with distaste a tone of bourgeois astonishment in my voice.

"I'm deeply sorry," she says.

"Don't be sorry. There's nothing to be sorry about. Why are you so sorry, anyway?" I try to speak in an ordinary voice, though with the naked Miss Goto a foot away it is hard to do so.

"I'm sorry about . . . sorry about . . ." She mumbles something.

We stand opposite each other in the dark room for about a minute. I know she is looking at me, but she has taken off her glasses and as at the temple I wonder how myopic she is. There are footfalls and voices in the lane outside. Miss Goto drops to the floor with the speed of a seasoned soldier.

"It's all right. No one can see if the lights are off. I'll draw the curtains, but the trouble is that with the curtains drawn the room will be stifling." I pull the curtains across the window by the bed and Miss Goto rises. I go to the "temple" window and draw the other curtain, making the room pitch dark. "Shall I turn on the light?"

"No." Miss Goto's voice is faint, but the negative is firm.

"I can't see a thing," I complain.

"I am . . . I am . . . on your bed."

I strip off my shirt and trousers, my vest and pants, and in a moment am lying beside Miss Goto. One of the advantages of Japan in the summer is that one wears very few clothes.

"No one will come?"

Kazumi enters my mind, but I say, "No."

It is a hot and sticky lovemaking accompanied by squelching sounds made each time our bodies part—sounds that are as much a Japanese summer noise as the crickets' cries. I am surprised to discover that clearly this isn't the first time Miss Goto has been to bed with a man; she knows what to do and does it fairly well. But her plainness (even in the dark, I can see it), her drink flush (her face is burning), her thinness (I can feel her bones), the contraceptive (a black one I bought one day in a sex shop when I was feeling low), all put me off, and I can't go through with it. I lose my excitement and I lie on my back and wish I had not begun the whole business. The turning fan plays tantalizingly up and down the bed; each part of the body—the feet, the thighs, the stomach, the chest, the face—longs for a cooling breeze to return. I enjoy this sensation more than that of having Miss Goto in my bed.

The doorbell rings. Although now there is a space between us, I can feel Miss Goto become tense.

"Who is it?" she asks.

"I don't know." I wonder if Kazumi has forgotten her key.

The bell rings again.

"What shall we do?"

"I'd better go and see."

"Shall I dress?"

"Yes."

I put on a yukata and go downstairs, but by the time I get to the front door the caller has gone. I return to the bedroom. Miss Goto is dressed. "I am sorry," she says. A few minutes after I see her out. "I am sorry," she says again and hurries off down the lane. I wonder who the caller was; anyway I am grateful to him for giving me an excuse to break off the unsuccessful lovemaking with Miss Goto. Whatever possessed me to lead her on? I hope she feels disillusioned about me and won't get in touch again.

 It was only eight when Miss Goto left. After scribbling in my bedroom for an hour, I decided for no particular reason to ring Noriko—perhaps I did so because the encounter with Miss Goto made me feel desolate. Why had she behaved so oddly? Why on one day behave like a scared virgin and on the next like a brazen hussy? The sad thing was that there was no one in the world with whom I could discuss her. Kazumi had not come home and I wanted to talk to someone. The fact that Noriko would be pleased to hear my voice was like an oasis, if not a very splendid one.

"Hello," I said.

"Oh, hello, Peter," she replied eagerly.

"How are you?"

"All right." Noriko always takes great care to pronounce these two words correctly, for I've often teased her about her lambdacisms.

"Is it hot in Tokyo?"

"Yes, it very hot." She said this with a tone of complaint in her voice. "By the way—"

"Yes?"

"It is O-Bon Festival next week. I have holiday. May I come down and see you?"

"I'm awfully busy, you know."

"I can help you."

"With my writing?"

"With housework."

"Kazumi does that."

"Is she there?"

"Off and on."

"You don't want me to come down." She sounded tearful.

I relented. "Of course I do. Love to see you, but oughtn't you to visit your parents?"

"It doesn't matter. You more important. I'll come on Wednesday."

God! As soon as that! "Let me know the time of your train."

"Right-ho! See you soon!"

Her "right-ho!" copied from me sounded absurd. What had I done? The frustrating and embarrassing incident with Miss Goto had driven me into inviting Noriko down here again. Oh dear!

No sooner had I gone upstairs than I heard the front door. Kazumi was back! I hurried down, trying not to look pleased to see her.

"I have been away," she said.

"Oh?"

"To see my sister." Was her "sister" Bob?

"Oh?" I made no further inquiry as I did not wish to be questioned about my activities. After she had gone to her room, had a shower, changed into her briefs, cooked some rice, I told her that Noriko was coming to stay. I told her this while she was lying on the bench seat, looking at television and chopsticking rice and pickles into her mouth.

"She must be very happy," Kazumi said.

"Yes, I think she is."

"She loves you very much."

"I know, I know, that's the trouble, too much."

"Why did you invite her?"

"She has a holiday for the O-Bon Festival, and I promised. But her coming doesn't mean you need go again. Will you stay while she is here this time?"

"Who was that Japanese woman you met outside the house?"

Stalling for time, I asked idiotically, "When?"

"Yesterday. She was wearing a kimono."

"Oh, that was Miss Goto, my ex-student. You met her with me at the Gion Shrine. Don't you remember?"

"Did you invite her here?"

"Yes, I did once for tea. I told you about it."

"I mean, did you invite her yesterday?"

"No, she invited me. She came here to fetch me to take me to have lunch with her mother and a Japanese professor I wanted to meet as he's interested in the Chinese philosophers I am trying to write about." How easy it was to lie! "The professor speaks no English so Miss Goto acted as interpreter. It was very useful meeting Professor Saito."

"You said you had lunch with Professor Watkins."

"Did I?" I was surprised at my own audacity.

"When I ask you if I make lunch for you, you say you have lunch with Professor Watkins at Kyoto Hotel."

"I can't have done! It must have been a mental aberration." Sometimes one can get away with murder if one uses a word one's interlocutor doesn't understand, because he or she, not wanting to appear ignorant will probably say, "Oh yes," and change the subject. I have played this trick on students, but Kazumi was too wily to be put off.

"You take lunch with that girl."

"With Miss Goto? Yes. I've just told you I did and with her mother and Professor Saito."

I had two trump cards left for I knew that Kazumi had not seen me at the Kyoto Hotel; by a hairbreadth she had missed doing so. I played one of my trumps. "Why did you have lunch with Professor

Watkins? He told me that you had lunch together at the Kyoto Hotel." But my question didn't unnerve her at all. She examined her rice bowl as if careful choice over which grain of cereal to have next were necessary and then said calmly, "Yes. I have lunch with Professor Watkins. He Oliver's friend. I know him for a long time. He like my uncle." Did Bob tell her to say this? "Oliver ask him to look after me. When you say you cannot lunch with me I am lonely. I telephone him and he ask me to have lunch with him at the Kyoto Hotel."

Overtrumped, I played my last card, but it was not an ace. "Why did you have lunch at the Kyoto Hotel?"

"Professor Watkins likes Kyoto Hotel very much. He always eat there. I have lunch with him many time at Kyoto Hotel."

This over-explanation smacked of unsureness. I had no more cards, though, and she had one, which she then played. "Where you lunch with Goto-san?"

"At the Royal," I lied quickly. Did her leaving out Mrs. Goto and the fictitious Professor Saito imply that she suspected I was trying to deceive her? "And her mother came too!" I added facetiously, but of course the reference was beyond her.

"I see." As if having made a difficult decision she chopsticked a ball of her glutinous rice into her mouth. She was pensive. She then went on. "Why you didn't tell me you lunch with Miss Goto, her mother, and Professor Saito?"

"When you came upstairs and suggested cooking lunch for me, I was in the middle of deep thought about my article, and I neither properly heard your question, nor properly answered it. I apparently said Professor Watkins without realizing it."

This seemed to satisfy her for she said, "I see," and put another ball of rice into her mouth.

I went back to my original question. "Will you stay on here while Noriko-san is here? Please do."

"Why do you want me to stay?"

"To keep her company."

"I have my own work."

"Yes, I know, but in the evening. I may have to go out sometimes. There's this professor Miss Goto has introduced me to and then a friend from England is coming soon."

"Oh?"

"Yes. Jack Tidmarsh. I shall have to spend some time with him," I lied. "You will stay won't you?"

She stretched out her chopsticks to nip up another piece of pickle from the dish on the occasional table, and clumsily I leaned forward and kissed the side of her hand. She withdrew her hand sharply, grazing the end of my nose with her chopsticks.

"Sorry," I said, obsequiously. I suddenly saw myself as a disreputable old lecher, and felt rather ashamed.

"I like Noriko-san," she said.

"Then stay."

"All right."

Kazumi did not ask any more questions about Miss Goto so I presumed she had accepted my explanation. Because she had agreed to stay during Noriko's visit, I felt I had won my duel with her. I was glad that she was going to stay for her presence in this house would save me from being smothered by affection. I did not tell her about my wife's arrival, for I was unaware of the exact date and hoped that Monica would not appear until after my return to Tokyo at the end of the month.

30

The girls' band is playing the Colonel Bogey march with laborious exactitude, turning it into a dirge. I am sitting at the desk in the bedroom with the fan trained directly onto my back trying to make notes for a series of lectures comparing Shakespeare's and Dryden's versions of the Cleopatra story. Misa-san is downstairs vacuum cleaning; two cicadas on the paulownia are screaming; the bean-curd man is sounding his horn; the main streets are reverberating with Monday's morning traffic. I am going to telephone Bob to sort of test him about Kazumi. She went off to work this morning as usual, but what did she do on Saturday night and on Sunday until she returned here at about ten p.m.?

The vacuum cleaner has stopped. Misa-san struggles up with

the cumbersome machine and after we have said twice to each other, "*Atsui desu ne!*" and "*So desu ne!*" I descend to telephone. I want to find out what I can about Bob and Kazumi. After one ring Bob answers in Japanese, "*Moshi, moshi?*"

"Peter here."

"Oh, hello. Was it you who rang yesterday? My wife told me—"

"Yes. Isn't it hot?"

"Yeah. Did you ring about the heat?"

"No. How's the drama coming along?" I find it hard to bring myself to the point.

"Fine, fine. You must come to a rehearsal."

"I'd love to. By the way . . ."

"Yeah?"

"Kazumi wasn't here on Saturday night."

"Oh?"

"Have you seen her?"

A pause.

"Yes, as a matter of fact I saw her Saturday lunchtime. She called me. She's quite an old friend, you know. I often saw her when she was living with the Olivers. I'm a sort of uncle to her."

I laugh.

"No, really. She's been here, met my wife; they get on."

"What did she want?"

"She wanted me to give her lunch at the Kyoto Hotel because you had told her that you were lunching there with me. I guessed it was subterfuge on your part. She expected you to turn up. Were you there?"

"Yes, I was lunching with Miss Goto."

"God! Her?"

"Yes. I like her."

"God! What was the idea of trying to deceive Kazumi?"

"I didn't want her to know about Miss Goto. Thought it better she shouldn't."

"I see."

"Sorry about all this, Bob."

"It cost me a lunch," he says, a bit regretfully.

"I'll make it up."

"You'd better."

Bob is a good chap. Perhaps he hasn't designs on Kazumi. He's just avuncular towards her.

"How did we miss you?" he asks.

I do not reveal the fact that I saw them entering the lift as we were descending the stairs. "Can't imagine. Perhaps we finished before you came. Why did Kazumi want to lunch with you at the Kyoto Hotel?"

"I've just told you, didn't you listen? Because she thought you were going to be there and she'd seen you meet a woman in kimono at the end of your lane."

"Can it be that she's jealous?"

"Maybe."

"Gives me encouragement."

"You're nuts. You certainly seem to be playing your cards cleverly. Are you working on the theory that to get one it's best to pretend to like another?"

"Yes." I hadn't thought I was, but since the idea is put into my mind I agree.

"Good luck to you then! Bye, I must fly." He rings off.

I remain seated on the floor, smiling to myself. I seem to have won a round. Kazumi is at least interested in whom I see and that can only be because she likes me, or did she promise to spy for Noriko? And Bob's "Good luck to you then!" Wasn't it a bit sarcastic, suggesting that I needed luck because he has her under his control?

31

Kyoto Station is swarming with people. Great marquees have been erected outside the main building to give shelter to the thousands who will wait for trains at this hectic, home-going time of the year. Not as many people go home for the O-Bon Festival, the All Soul's Day, as they do at the New Year, but O-Bon has become a sort of August Bank Holiday and trains are packed with home-visiting travelers and with those, like Noriko, who are taking a few days off. I have never known Kyoto Station abandoned; whenever I

have been there it has always been crowded; this afternoon, it is
absolutely jammed. There are queues by the telephones, many waiting to have their shoes cleaned, hundreds in line by the ticket office,
scores wanting taxis, groups arriving in motorcars at every moment.
I am early for Noriko's train—guilt makes me early? An hour ahead
of time.

The department-store section of the station is alive with shoppers, would-be shoppers, travelers enjoying the air-conditioned
coolness, and there is not a free table in any of the restaurants. I
leave the station and seek refuge in the cool, darkened bar of an
American-style hotel, a welcome haven from the heat and the
crowds. I order a beer from a somnolent barman and wish I did not
have to meet Noriko. I wish I were staying at this comfortable place
where I should not have to cope with the immediate problem of living. I am tempted to take a room and move in.

I do my best when Noriko arrives, but I know she senses that
my "warm" welcome is feigned. In the taxi, I say with the intention
of forestalling a question, "I've asked Kazumi-san to stay on in the
house while you're here."

"Yes," Noriko replies, without any sign of objection or disappointment. She is so excited at coming to Kyoto that if I had told
her that I had given up the house and was sleeping on the pavement, her "yes" would have had the same intonation, or that is what
I think.

"Also," I warn, "an English friend is arriving this week and I
shall have to look after him." I decide that I shall not tell Noriko
about Monica yet.

"Can't I help you?"

"Better not. He is a friend of my wife."

As always when I give this reason for her exclusion, she says
resignedly, "I see."

I move my hand from my lap to the seat and at once she covers
it with hers; when I disengage my hand a few moments later, she
says, "Why?"

"It's so hot."

"Oh." She makes a little petulant noise.

Kazumi is in when we arrive and the two women greet each

other like fond sisters who have not met for years, nattering away very fast in Japanese. I feel out of it. They sit on the bench seats and become completely absorbed in each other.

I say quite loudly in English, "I'll go and prepare supper."

They continue to talk.

I repeat my statement.

Noriko gives me the exasperated glance of a mother who has been interrupted for the ninth time by her fractious child. "What?"

"I said I'd go and get the supper ready."

"All right, darling." She turns back to Kazumi and her conversation.

"Would you like to go upstairs to the bedroom?" I ask Noriko.

"What did you say?"

I repeat my question.

She looks at Kazumi. "It is so hot. I think I shall sleep downstairs."

"Here?"

"In the other room."

"The moon-viewing room? But that is the hottest room in the house, and there are no mosquito screens—"

"Kazumi-san says she will lend me her fan and there is the mosquito stuff."

"But what will Kazumi-san do without a fan?"

Kazumi explains that she has brought a fan from her apartment.

I repair to the kitchen and start making a risotto. I pour myself a stiff whiskey. What is Kazumi up to? I stir the risotto angrily while the women twitter away in the next room, and then, with a suffering look on my face, I slide open the kitchen door, go heavily down on my knees in the dining recess, and begin to lay the table. Noriko gives that "mother's" glance again and turns back to Kazumi.

I address Noriko, not Kazumi of whom I am shy, "Would you like to help?"

"Sorry, darling."

That awful "darling"! Noriko comes to the table, but she has a cigarette dangling from her lips, and she keeps on talking in Japanese as she half-heartedly helps. I can understand enough of their conversation to tell that it is just silly female chatter about the heat, people in Noriko's office, she-said-I-said stuff. Noriko seems to amuse

Kazumi, but I am unable to grasp the point of her jokes. She never says anything funny to me.

The two women sit opposite each other at supper and when I put the risotto down saying, proudly, "See what I've made for you!" they laugh. The telephone rings. Kazumi leans sideways to answer, but I twist round and pick up the receiver first. It is Miss Goto. I hold the earpiece close to my ear hoping that the caller's voice cannot be heard; for once I am grateful for Miss Goto's murmur.

"How wonderful to hear your voice, Jack!" I say. "When did you arrive?"

"This is Miss Goto."

"Only just got in? Hotel all right?"

"Is that you, Mr. Meadowes?"

"Yes, it is hot, isn't it?"

"It is Miss Goto."

"I'll come and see you this evening."

"To my house? No, Mr. Meadowes, I—"

"At the Kyoto Hotel."

I don't want to see Miss Goto. "Yes, in about an hour. I'll meet you at the bar."

"The bar, Mr. Meadowes?"

"In the lobby, then. Bye for now, Jack."

I ring off quickly. Noriko and Kazumi have begun another of their conversations and neither of them gives me the inquiring look I expected and almost wanted.

"Is the risotto good?" I ask.

They both giggle.

"Well, is it?"

They go on giggling.

"What's so funny?"

Noriko begins, "Kazumi-san say, Kazumi-san say—" The rest of her sentence is drowned in laughter.

"What does Kazumi-san say?" I glare at Kazumi.

"Nothing."

Noriko splutters. "Kazumi-san say that the risotto is like—," she splutters more—"is like, is like *okayu*." She puts a hand over her mouth and rocks with laughter.

"Oh?"

They both become convulsed with merriment.

Okayu is a gruel made of rice and water with a little salt. It tastes quite nasty and is given for a stomach ache.

32 After breakfast Kazumi announces that she is going to the cemetery to clean her mother's grave as it is the first day of O-Bon. Noriko says that she is going with her. I should have refused had I been asked to accompany them, but Kazumi does not invite me. I should have liked to be asked. The two go off together merrily with a plastic basket, cleaning powder, and a scrubbing brush; they seem more about a jovial task than a mournful one in a graveyard, but although the O-Bon Festival commemorates those who have died in the family, it is not a sad occasion. In the courtyards of village temples, the villagers in *yukata* perform the O-Bon dance wearing bands round their heads.

Last evening when I saw Miss Goto at the Kyoto Hotel, she again mentioned the Daimonji bonfires and suggested that we might view them together. "I know a good place," she said, dubiously. I explained that a friend of mine had arrived from England and that I would not be free. Miss Goto was puzzled about the way I had spoken to her on the telephone.

"You called me Jack."

"Did I? This friend of mine's name is Jack."

"I see."

"I thought it was he when you rang. I was expecting him to telephone."

It was difficult to get rid of Miss Goto. I got the impression that she had fallen for me, in spite of my inadequacy, for when I told her that she couldn't come home as the landlady had returned to the main house and she might be seen, she actually proposed our slipping off to the *abekku* hotel for an hour or two, and I couldn't get away without promising to go with her to the drama festival. She obviously wants to try it with me again, and she probably thinks that it was her fault, or that the ring of the doorbell put me off.

Thinking of the two Japanese women with whom I am at present involved, and the one with whom I'd like to be involved but who won't let me be, makes me want to escape from them all. I telephone Bob.

"Why hello there!"

"Isn't it hot?" I say, fatuously.

"It was ninety-eight yesterday."

"What are you doing about the Daimonji Festival?"

"Precisely nothing. I have seen it before, you know, in the twenty years I've been here. You can see the fires from the roof of this house as well as you can from anywhere, but I don't think I've been up to look at them for the last five years. My wife watches them every year."

"Are you going to be in, Bob?"

"I'll say I am! We're having a rehearsal tonight."

"Rehearsal?"

"*Kagotsurube*, the Kabuki play. We're doing it for the drama festival. I told you about it the other day."

"Oh, yes, so you did." I had forgotten.

"We do a Western drama one year and a Japanese classic the next. Last year we did *Lady Windermere's Fan*, so this year it's Kabuki. I hope you're coming to see it."

"Of course. Miss Goto is getting tickets. What time is the rehearsal and where is it?"

"It's here, after our meal. Seven."

"Could I come round?"

"Sure."

"I want to escape from this house. Noriko is here and Kazumi has a holiday because of O-Bon. All the time they tittle-tattle away together in Japanese and I can't—"

Bob laughs. "My!"

"At any moment Miss Goto will ring up and ask to come round. And there's my wife—"

"She here, too?"

"No, but she may be soon."

"Come at six. We'll eat. Then you can watch the rehearsal. You might have some helpful suggestions. Helpful, mind!"

Kazumi and Noriko return from the cemetery much sooner than I expected them to. I imagined that the tomb-scrubbing ritual would take them at least all the morning, but they come in at half past ten while I am working at the desk upstairs. Noriko immediately ascends. Then she stands behind me and puts her arms round my neck.

"You're screening me from the fan."

She moves. "Darling, where will we go to see the Daimonji? Kazumi-san says that—"

"I'm afraid that I shan't be able to go with you as I must see this English friend."

"You saw him last night."

"Only for a very short time." I was less than half an hour in the hotel with Miss Goto.

"Must you see him tonight?"

"I'm afraid I must. It's a great bore but I must."

"Why?"

"He's an old friend and I promised. You can go out with Kazumi-san tonight."

"She's going to see some friends."

"Oh?"

"Yes. Can't I come with you, darling?"

"Sorry."

"I shall be alone."

"I shan't be late."

"But, darling, you—"

The telephone rings. I jump up.

Noriko is at the head of the stairs before me. I want to answer it for I am sure it is Miss Goto, but Noriko nimbly descends the stairs and is kneeling by the instrument several seconds before I arrive.

"It's for you. Miss Goto."

"Say I'm out," I whisper.

Noriko shakes her head and holds the receiver towards me. I sit on the floor and take the receiver from Noriko, who stays by my side, almost on top of me.

"Good morning, Miss Goto. How have you been? What a hot summer we're having!"

"Mr. Meadowes, may I come and see you? In the daytime it wouldn't matter about the person in the main house; there would be no need for us to put on any lights so she wouldn't know if anyone was there or not. I have a holiday and—"

"Just a minute please, Miss Goto." I put my hand over the speaking piece. "Noriko," I whisper, "upstairs on my desk is a red exercise book. Could you fetch it, please?"

"What?"

"A red exercise book on my desk or somewhere."

"All right." Noriko goes upstairs.

I speak into the phone. "I'm sorry, Miss Goto, but today is impossible. I told you last night, some students from Tokyo have just arrived and I'm rather taken up with them."

Flatly, Miss Goto replies, "You seem to be very busy with your friend from England and now your students." Is there a hint of disbelief in her voice?

"I am busy. Yes, I am. I wish I weren't."

"Who answered the telephone?"

I am surprised by the directness of Miss Goto's tone, but once one has been to bed with someone their attitude changes, even if the bedding has been unsuccessful. I suppose Miss Goto feels that now she has rights, a claim on me, or does she blame herself for the failure and want to try again? "The maid," I say.

Noriko comes down from the bedroom crying, "I cannot find, Peter. It is not on the desk."

"Who is that?" asks Miss Goto.

"Just a minute, please, Miss Goto. So sorry."

Noriko is by my side. "I cannot find." She is breathing hard and there are pearls of sweat on the top of her nose.

"Never mind," I say. There is no red exercise book, of course; all my notebooks are the gray, standard Japanese ones. "I'm awfully sorry, Miss Goto, I cannot find the information you want at the moment, but if you could telephone in a day or two—"

Almost angrily, Miss Goto interrupts, "But Mr. Meadowes, what about the drama festival? It is on Saturday. I have two tickets, and—"

"Please telephone tomorrow morning. I can't talk now," I snap crossly and bang down the receiver while Miss Goto is saying, "But Mr. Meadowes . . ." I turn to Noriko. "Oh curse these students! Even in Kyoto they bother one."

"Is Miss Goto one of your students?"

"She was," I answer truthfully. "Now she is here, doing secretarial work, but she still keeps up an interest in English literature. She is very good at English." This is a dig at Noriko, whose knowledge of English is not literary; she has always envied those who could speak about English writers.

"Is she beautiful?"

"Not at all."

"Are you sure?"

"If you saw her, you wouldn't doubt my word." The advantage of being unfaithful with an unbeautiful person is that you will not be suspected.

"Do you love her?"

"No."

"Are you sure?"

"Yes."

I have had this sort of interrogation dozens of times with Noriko. It always ends the same way.

She says, "I believe you, darling," looking as if she doesn't.

I say, "You are silly, you know."

She says, "Yes, I know. I am very silly."

And either we lapse into silence or talk of something else. This time Noriko returns to the subject of the Daimonji Festival, which she wants to see with me. I had intended to get away soon after lunch and go to a cinema before it was time to visit Bob, but I am forced into making a compromise and staying with Noriko until five o'clock. Kazumi goes out before lunch and so Noriko and I are on our own. It is strange how different she is when we are alone from when we are in the company of other Japanese women. With me she is solemn, submissive, dull—as she is now; with them, she is bright, vivacious, as she was with Kazumi last evening.

33 Mrs. Watkins goes right down on the *genkan* step, her head almost touching the floor while she mutters words of welcome. That she is wearing a kimono of somber hue appropriate to her matronly years does not surprise me, for I had heard she always wore Japanese dress, but the fact that she is so completely the typical, old-fashioned, middle-aged, middle-class Japanese housewife without a trace of Americanization does. Bob told me that she was not like an American wife, but I did not expect her to be so un-westernized. Mrs. Watkins's straight, gray-black hair is divided into a central parting and sleeked back into a bun; she has no make-up and her expression is kindly, but the lines around her eyes and mouth suggest either illness or anxiety or strain. It does not astonish me that Bob occasionally stays out all night. I wonder if she is older than Bob; she does not look younger.

"Professor Watkins?"

"Professor Watkins is expecting you," she says like a prewar English parlormaid.

I take off my shoes and follow her down a passage. She taps a sliding door. "*Gomen nasai.*"

"*Hai?*" comes Bob's voice from the other side of the fusuma.

Mrs. Watkins opens one of the doors. "*Meadowes-sensei ga irasshaimashita.*"

Bob, in nothing but spectacles and a pair of shorts, is sitting on the floor, which is matted with tatami, at a low Japanese table and reclining against a canvas backrest. He has a glass of whiskey in his hand; in front of him is a half-empty bottle of Suntory and an ice bucket; behind him whirl two standard fans. There are no books on the table, or even on the floor; his sole occupation seems to be drinking whiskey. The room, which gives onto a small garden, is cool. "Hello, Peter," he says. "Excuse my not getting up." His wife comes after me into the large room, takes a cushion from a pile of four in a corner and places it punctiliously by the table opposite Bob. "*Dozo,*" she says.

I lower myself onto the cushion and face Bob. Mrs. Watkins flutters out of the room.

"We'll have to eat soon," Bob warns, "as these goddamned students will be here for the rehearsal. I don't know why I go in for this drama festival." He sighs. His eyes are bloodshot and his voice is a bit slurred. I wonder if he has drunk half the bottle of Suntory during the afternoon. It occurs to me for the first time that perhaps Bob solves his expatriate problem by drinking heavily.

"You know you enjoy the drama festival," I say.

"Enjoy it? Like hell I enjoy it! Have a drink. There's no glass. I told her you were coming." He bangs the table and shouts, "Junko!" Then he laughs a little wildly and says, "Having trouble with Yatsuhashi, the grand courtesan. Do you know the play?"

"Isn't it about a pockmarked countryman who is wealthy and visits the Yoshiwara district of Edo and falls for the most glamorous whore in the quarter?" I remember I have had this conversation with Bob before.

"Whore? Well, she is a whore, but courtesan is the correct word."

"A euphemism?"

"Yes, if you like, but I prefer it," Bob rather snapped.

"And the courtesan plays the wretched farmer along, but prefers her lover?"

"Yes. That's about it."

Mrs. Watkins enters noiselessly with a loaded tray and kneels by the table. Bob takes no notice of her. She places a plate of cold ham, salad, and floury boiled potatoes in front of each of us, murmuring, "Dozo." It is like service in a Japanese inn, except that the "maid" is even more unobtrusive than usual. One look at my plate makes me understand why Bob often dines out. I am anxious to talk about Noriko and my predicament. Discussing the play doesn't interest me in the least. Mrs. Watkins comes in again; this time with a glass. Bob pours me a whiskey. "I hope you don't mind drinking with your meal. I'm afraid that the players will be here at any minute and we must hurry. I did warn you."

"That's quite all right." I don't have a chance to broach my subject for Bob will go on about his play. He never more than grunts at Mrs. Watkins and I begin to wonder whether I have been right in assuming that the woman who serves us is his wife. He calls her Junko, a girl's name, so she could be a maid, but she must be his wife. How different she is from Kazumi! Bob mentioned once, though, that his wife was a good cook and the meal (a carelessly made lemon pie follows the ham) is far below the Prince élu des Gastronomes' standards. Perhaps the story I heard from someone that she was his former cook was erroneous, or she may be an expert at Japanese dishes and Bob ordered Western-style food because I was coming. When Bob eats out, however, he usually goes to Western-style restaurants. I envy Bob this apparent paragon of a helpmeet (among whose qualities seems to be the inestimable one of silence) and laugh at the thought of Monica treating me like a feudal lord. Even Noriko wouldn't conform to such an extent.

"What's funny?" asks Bob, curtly.

"Nothing. I was thinking that Noriko would never be so—"

"So what?" Bob seems a different person at home, so domineering. I'm not sure which is his true self: the overbearing character he now seems to be or the easygoing American expatriate I have met before. Certainly, he is master in his own house. Perhaps the impending rehearsal has put him into this fractious mood.

"Nothing," I reply. "By the way, where do you think Kazumi went on Saturday night?"

"How do I know?" Is Bob lying?

The doorbell rings.

Bob yells, "Junko!" And almost at once Mrs. Watkins enters with a *yukata*. Bob stands up and his wife helps him into the cotton kimono, a white one with a bold black pattern, and then she winds the sash round his waist carefully tying the bow at the back. "Hurry," he says, lifting his feet up and down impatiently.

The doorbell rings again. Japanese students can be exacting.

Mrs. Watkins trips off to the *genkan* and soon the flimsy little house rocks with young men and women dressed in summer garb and carrying dog-eared texts of the play. They are well-behaved though and treat Bob, whom they call Watkins-sensei, with respect, obeying his strident commands as promptly as recruits.

The scene shifters move the table, the cushions, and the fans and help Mrs. Watkins carry out the supper things, then Bob claps his hands and parades the actors, the actresses, the prompters, the scene shifters, the three assistant directors, the four stage managers, the program makers. There must be seventy people connected with the play and large though the room is, it is only just big enough to contain them all. Bob leads them in a series of physical exercises, which, because of the lack of space, they perform more earnestly than skillfully. I am distressed but not surprised to notice that none of the students sniggers at their outsize, perspiring, red-in-the-face foreign teacher, grotesque in his kimono; there are no smiles when students inadvertently kick, hit, or bump one another. There is no larking. This absurd "warming up to get in the right mood" is taken with alarming seriousness. One of the assistant directors blows a whistle, Bob shouts, "Places!" and there is a scramble as the "set" is arranged.

Bob says, "Now this evening we have the honor of the presence of Professor Meadowes from Tokyo. He is English, so he will be able to put us right over our pronunciation of the English language." Bob pauses for a laugh that doesn't come, and then adds, "And other things." All eyes turn in my direction, but they soon switch away when Bob cries, "Curtain!" The first assistant producer claps his hands and the diminutive mistress of the teahouse welcomes Jiro, the pockmarked countryman, and his two friends. "You are most welcome, please come in. We have been talking about you; the courtesan Yatsuhashi will be here shortly."

"O.K.," says Bob. "Cut to Yatsuhashi's entrance."

A girl dressed in a T-shirt and brief shorts struts slowly onto the "set." She is followed by three female attendants who flutter around her. The courtesan gradually lowers herself and sits on her heels next to Jiro, bows to him and his friends, who delightedly return the greeting. The friends utter words of praise. One of them says, "Here, here, you must not praise her so much. If you do, Jiro will become jealous."

JIRO: (*a tall, handsome, innocent-looking young man with a mop of hair. He is quite unlike the character, whose scarred face is supposed to make him repellent. The student knows his part but speaks his lines as if dictating a cable.*) Why not at all. She is, after all, for sale. The days I am not using her, pray buy her yourselves.

YATSUHASHI: (*in a playful, precious tone*) Oh, what hateful things you do say! If a guest appears whom I do not like, then I myself do not appear. (*She gives a smug grimace.*)

The actress playing the part of the courtesan takes a ball-point pen from the top of her T-shirt and touches Jiro's hand with it. The pen represents a long-stemmed pipe whose little bowl is hot, so it is supposed to burn him, but the young actor's reactions are slow and he does not withdraw his hand quickly enough.

Bob interrupts: "No, no, NO! Jiro, you have been burnt. You must snatch your hand away, say, "Ow, that hurt!" if you like—it's not in the script, but Kabuki actors often put in extra words of their own. Let's do that bit again. Yatsuhashi!"

"Yes, Professor Watkins?"

"Where's your pipe?"

"I did not bring."

"I did not bring it," corrects Bob, forever the teacher. "But it's not your responsibility to bring it. Property man!"

"Yes, Professor Watkins?" says a small young man with a pale, round face and black-rimmed glasses.

"Why didn't you bring Yatsuhashi's pipe?"

While Bob is remonstrating with the property man and then making the players repeat the scene, my thoughts turn to Kazumi. In a way she resembles Yatsuhashi, who is cruel and may not care for Jiro. When she spitefully burns him with the bowl of her pipe he does not complain, just as I probably would not complain if Kazumi burnt me. Jiro's spots are supposed to make him unattractive, just as my paunch must make me undesirable to most; not to Noriko, though (with her I can stick it out, let it make a gap in the front of my shirt), nor to Miss Goto, it seems, but to Kazumi?

The rehearsal continues. It is now the scene between Yatsu-hashi and Einojo, her real lover, who accuses her of being heartless. He tells her that unless she formally refuses Jiro's offer to buy her out of her bond to the teahouse, he will have nothing more to do with her.

"Now we come to the big scene, Peter," says Bob.

I have been daydreaming about Kazumi and others and looking out of the window at a gnarled, stunted, twisted pine on the lawn.

"Now we come to the big scene, Peter," repeats Bob, rather querulously.

"Oh, yes?"

"I'd like you to watch it closely. And if you have any ideas, please shout. Now, let's begin with Yatsuhashi's big speech. There are two ways of interpreting this: that she dislikes Jiro; that she's only pretending to dislike him. We are going to do it the first way, for my reading of the character of Ka—, I mean Yatsuhashi, is that she hates him and has only been getting what she can out of him."

I am amazed. Was it "Kazumi" that he nearly said or just a slip of the tongue? Is Bob also thinking about my relationship with Kazumi?

"Now, come, Yatsuhashi, begin," says Bob. "And be angry, spit fire!"

> YATSUHASHI: *(in a meek little voice)* For some time I have been contemplating refusal . . .

She goes on, but does not get worked up at the end of her speech when she says, "And it is now that I take the opportunity to decline and to respectfully request that you see me no more."

Bob holds up his hands. "No, no, NO! More fire. Let me show you." I feel that he has been longing to do this. Bob moves to the middle of the room and reads in a hoarse falsetto the speech, working up to a crescendo, jugular veins bulging, eyes popping, face reddening when he gets to, "And now I take the opportunity to decline and to respectfully request that you see me no more."

Rather mild words for such rage, I feel, but I only say, "There's just one thing, Bob?"

"Yes?" he asks fiercely.

"I don't much like the split infinitive 'to respectfully request'; couldn't you say 'and with respect I ask you to see me no more'?"

"No. We could not. The script says 'to respectfully request.' We mustn't change it."

I do not ask why the clumsy lines should not be changed and simply add, "Your rage was good, Bob." I feel as if I have fawned, for I think the words should be said coolly.

Jiro then loses face in front of his companions. This is serious and is to have dire consequences, but in the present scene he maintains his self-control and speaks eloquently. The young, lanky student doesn't do too badly and says with feeling the last lines, "It would be but decent, think, courtesan, to consider my honor as a man." But

Bob jumps up with, "More pathos, Jiro. Pathos. You must wring the hearts of the audience here." With sobs in his throat Bob repeats the lines, breaking down at the end which, I feel, is not what the author intended. I think he meant Jiro to be calm, obviously deeply hurt, but calm. However, the student obeys his teacher and imitates him by overacting and thus spoiling the lines, but Bob is pleased.

I am reminded of Kazumi again at the end of the scene when, after Yatsuhashi has left, Jiro says to the mistress of the teahouse, "To be so thrown over, yet to happily return home; indeed, one knows not what kind of fool to call me." The student says these words quietly, but Bob will make him rant and the young man can't or doesn't feel it is right to. I wonder how he will play it on the night.

In the final scene Jiro gets his revenge. Four months late he returns from the country, goes to the teahouse, and summons Yatsuhashi, who appears. He suggests that they have a new beginning and asks her to treat him as a new guest. Yatsuhashi accepts a cup of sake from Jiro—a sign of reconciliation—and he tells her it is a farewell cup. She tries to rise. He steps on her kimono and says, " . . . you shamed me in the very midst of my love." And a few moments later, after saying, "How you have humiliated me!" he kills her with his sword.

"Oh Yatsuhashi!" moans Bob. "Why do you come to rehearsal in those ridiculous clothes? Jiro has to tread on your kimono to prevent you from rising. This move needs practicing. But how can Jiro step onto those tight shorts? I'll get a kimono." Bob leaves the room. Yatsuhashi looks ashamed. Jim practices treading on the imaginary kimono.

It is a moving scene, if done well. I must say it sounds better in Japanese than it does in English, in the same way that Italian opera sounds better in the original than when translated.

The point of the play, or one of them, is that it is uncertain whether Yatsuhashi loves poor, ugly Jiro or not. She's caught in the mesh made by her "owner," her lover, and the teahouse mistress just as Kazumi is perhaps caught up in her obligation to Oliver, to Bob, and perhaps to Mr. Ohno. In Japan obligations count and it's hard to get out of them. Probably Yatsuhashi has a soft spot for the repulsive Jiro, who has squandered a lot of money on her; possibly Kazumi has a soft spot for me. But I want more than that. So does Jiro.

Bob returns with one of his wife's kimonos and a sash. "Now let's try that scene again."

They do, and Jiro duly dispatches Yatsuhashi with a wooden sword. He then polishes off the maid, who arrives with a lamp. His final words are, "Ah—sword—you—cut—well!" And these are followed by a challenging stance and the making of a grimace. These are conventional Kabuki gestures and the student does not do them with aplomb. Bob naturally notices this and he, of course, shows the lad how to do it. In spite of the fact that Bob's posture and grimace are grotesque and very funny, no one, except me (I fail to stifle a laugh) gives so much as a faint smile; all are solemn, and the young man nods gravely and then tries to copy his teacher.

I can bear no more. I slide open a fusuma and slip into the passage.

I admire Bob for taking this amateur production seriously; the way he throws himself into it and makes it important to him and to those taking part is commendable. I know he likes the zealous, humorless, determined attitude of the students; no doubt it confirms his belief in what he is doing, gives him a sense of accomplishment. If anyone told him he was wasting his time, he'd say, "Wasting my time? What do you mean? Doing this play will be an experience that these students will never forget, and besides they learn a lot of English during the rehearsals. I always speak English during the rehearsals." Bob has something of Mr. Chips about him, but then so does every successful teacher.

34

I go down the passage to the kitchen where I find Mrs. Watkins mixing orange cordial in a huge jug. She jumps like a startled hen when she sees me, as if I had caught her concocting some nefarious brew. She recovers quickly and smiles. She has a sweet face: her swept-back hair, her thick, arched eyebrows, her dark, sad eyes, her pale complexion give her a saintly, pre-Raphaelite look, which would be hard to live up to. I tell her I want to see the Daimonji bonfires and she leads me up to the first floor and then up a steep flight of steps to a sort of platform on the roof from where there is a good view of the hills. It is past dusk and the hills are deep, dark silhouettes against the sky.

"Soon they light the fires. I come back." She goes. From below comes Bob's yell, "Ah—sword—you—now pause for effect—cut—pause again and then let them have it—WELL!" Presently, the bonfires come alight. The largest and the nearest is the *dai* ("big"), and on the other hills there is a boat, which never gets going properly, the ideogram for "law," and another *dai*. Mrs. Watkins returns and excitedly points out the fires; childlike she is in her enjoyment of them. I feel sorry for her, such a slave she seems to be, so entirely under the thumb of Bob the autocrat, and autocrat he decidedly is at home, and in the classroom too, judging by his attitude to his students. Mrs. Watkins's English is quite adequate and I talk to her on the roof while we watch the fires, trying to find out a little about her life with Bob. Their children, a son of fifteen, and a daughter of thirteen, are both being educated in Japanese schools; at the moment they are away at a summer camp in the mountains.

"Have you been to the States?" I ask, rather impertinently.

"No."

"Don't you go when your husband goes?"

"No."

"Wouldn't you like to go?"

"I don't know."

"You ought to tell him to take you next time he goes," I say, teasingly. "It is rather unfair of him not to take you. Don't you get bored with Kyoto?"

Mrs. Watkins does not reply. She is too loyal to indulge in talk that even lightly hints censure of Bob. Her silence is a rebuke. We sit without speaking, watching the ideograms and the boat slowly disintegrate as the fires extinguish themselves, until Bob shouts, "Junko! Junko!" At once, Mrs. Watkins descends. I stay, gazing at the dying fires and wondering if Bob has not got the best of both worlds and solved the expatriate problem. But, I tell myself, he has limited his horizons.

A rowdy chorus of unmusical voices rouses me and down the stairs I go to find Bob and his students singing their university song.

They have linked arms and formed a sort of circle, as far as it is possible for such a large group to do so in the room. With their faces hot and contorted, brows furrowed, voices passionate and raucous, they are something between Fascist Youth and the Lions' Club. Bob, with Yatsuhashi on one side and Jiro on the other, bawls more loudly than anyone the trite words of the anthem, whose every verse ends with eight repetitions of the university's name. When the name has been shouted for the last time and the subsequent applause and *banzais* are over, the students leave politely and in good order.

Bob, flushed and perspiring, says, "Thank the Lord they've gone! Let's have a drink. Junko!"

We settle down on the floor again, after Mrs. Watkins has put the table and the cushions back into the center of the room; and while she clears away glasses and plates that have been left all over the place by the students, we drink whiskey.

"The rehearsal went well, I thought," I say.

"You left before we got going. Japanese students have to warm up."

"It was so hot in this room and I wanted to see the bonfires. Your wife . . ." I look round at Mrs. Watkins, who is kneeling on the floor and loading a tray with glasses, but she seems engrossed in her task and not to have heard. "Your wife showed them to me. There was a splendid view from the roof."

"Hmm." Bob is not interested.

"Did Jiro get his curtain line right?"

"Why did you laugh?"

"I, er, I laughed at your Kabuki attitudes. They were quite superb. Your *mie* was excellent."

"Better than the boy's, eh? He's too timid. He doesn't see the point of the part. He doesn't see the part as I see it. We'll have to have a conference about it. Let's go out. Junko, *sanpo ni ikimasu.*"

"*Hai.*"

Mrs. Watkins puts down the heavy tray, which she has just lifted from the floor with a visible effort, and follows Bob out of the room. In a few minutes the master of the house reappears dressed in sportshirt and slacks and soon he and I are walking down the lane to the main road, where we take a taxi into town.

"I wished you'd stayed longer for the rehearsal. You might have had some ideas."

"I wanted to see the fires and I know nothing about Kabuki."

"The fires!" says Bob, scornfully.

Just as we have passed the Kyoto Hotel and are entering the busy part of Kawaramachi, I see, walking among the throngs of sightseers and looking lost and dejected, Noriko.

"There's Noriko!"

"Where?" asks Bob.

"Back there."

"D'you want to stop?"

"No." I wish I hadn't seen her.

We get out of our taxi farther down the street and go up an alley gaily lit with bar signs; it is like a lane in fairyland. I hurry ahead, fearing that Noriko might see me. Boys in white shirts and black bow ties try to entice us into their bars with traffic policeman signals.

"It's too hot to rush," cries Bob.

"I don't want Noriko to see me."

"She's right at the other end of Kawaramachi."

I turn round to Bob, who is walking behind me in the narrow lane of blazing bar names. "She looked so lonely in the crowd."

"Japan is full of lonely people in the crowd. Where lonelier can one be? If you feel contrite, go back and meet her."

For a moment I think of walking back up the main street to find Noriko, knowing how pleased she would be to see me, but I don't. I go with Bob to a bar which for him is like a club in that he is warmly welcomed by the barmaids—not an automatic professional greeting at all—and the customers. The bar is tiny; a box at the end of a passage off the alley, the size of a small bedroom. The customers are men, but behind the bar stand three girls.

"Do you come here often?" I ask.

"Two or three times a week. Some play bridge, others go to mah-jong parlors, I relax in this bar."

"What about your—?"

"My wife?"

"Doesn't she—?"

"No, she doesn't. I thought I told you she's Japanese style. Japanese wives don't mind their husbands going out on their own. It's the custom here. You must know that. My wife would be surprised if I didn't go out and—what do you think of Ta-chan?"

"Who?"

"That girl behind the bar."

I look towards the bar, meet Ta-chan's steady, dark eyes, and then look away. I am not interested in bargirls.

"Oh," says Bob, "I was going to ask you, where did you go with Miss Goto after the lunch you gave her at the Kyoto Hotel?"

"To a temple. And then I took her to an *abekku* hotel, but she ran away while I was in the bath."

Bob roars with rather mocking laughter, so I do not relate to him the sequence. He begins to talk in Japanese to one of the men at the bar. I can't hear what he is saying because of the blaring rock music, but I can tell by the glances that the man keeps giving me that Bob is telling him my story about Miss Goto and the hotel. I mind; it is silly of me, but I do.

I get up to leave. "I must go."

"You can't go until you have danced with Ta-chan," teases Bob. "She's a sweet girl. Ta-chan, my friend wants to dance with you."

"No, Bob," I protest. I have no desire to dance.

"I'll dance with her then." Perhaps this is what he has been wanting to do. In the tiny space behind the barstools Bob puts his arms round Ta-chan and they sway together quite out of time with the rock number the cassette machine is playing. The tape ends and Bob releases the bar hostess and resumes his seat by me. "You know, Peter, it's a relief to come here to chat with friends, with Mama-san, with the girls. One can say what one likes. You know these hostesses have a—how shall I put it?—a sympathetic ear. Now Mama-san—" He turns to the bar. "Ta-chan!"

"*Hai?*" Ta-chan sings out smartly and cheerily.

"*Mama-san itsu kaette kimasu ka?*"

"*Mo sugu.*"

"She'll be here soon. Have another drink. Ta-chan, whiskey *nihai kudasai.*" Bob is pleased to show off his Japanese and his intimacy with the bargirls. I am getting drunk—Bob has got to the stage when one more drink makes little difference—and when the whiskey comes I drink mine quickly as I wish to leave. If I don't envy Bob's choice of partner, I do envy his ability to be both tied and independent at the same time. It seems illogical that he is freer than I.

"How do you manage it, Bob?"

"In Japan it is possible, provided you pick the right sort of wife." He waggles a finger at me. "The right sort, understand? Not the kind that has been contaminated with Western ideas. At home I have respect, affection, obedience, care—naturally she does all the domestic chores, and without so much as a squeak of complaint; here I get, well, titillation, and, if I want it, sex."

"I must go, Bob."

"Back to dreary Noriko?"

Charitably I put his sarcasm down to the whiskeys he has drunk.

Ta-chan has come out from behind the bar and is standing by the door.

"You go?" she asks, face expectant.

"Yes."

"I lonely."

I shake my head.

"I come with you?"

"No, sorry."

"Please come again."

I push past her and stagger out of the bar down the passagelike alley bumping into the doors of bars on either side until I reach a wider alley, cross a bridge over a rushing brook, and march studiously up the street. There are many people about; drunks are swaying; hostesses are bowing inebriated customers into taxis; sober young men, filled only with Coca-Cola, are hurrying towards the interurban train that will take them to Osaka; other young men are linked together and singing. It is after midnight, yet the city is alive. I stop at a fruit shop and buy a Hawaiian pineapple, and then I cross Sanjo Bridge unsteadily and go up Sanjo Street. Another fruit shop is open and I buy some peaches, and with a paper bag on each arm I arrive merrily at the head of my lane. Noriko is slumped on the doorstep.

"What's the matter?"

"I forget my key."

"Kazumi not back?" I hand her my parcels, which she takes automatically.

"No."

"How long have you—?"

"Two hours."

"God!"

In the sitting room she narrows her eyes and says, "I am a little angry."

"Oh, why?"

"You said you wouldn't be late."

I look at my watch. "It's only a quarter to one."

"Where have you been?"

"With my friend."

"Who is he?"

"From England. I told you."

"Where did you go?"

"Just chatting in the Kyoto Hotel."

"I went to the Kyoto Hotel and did not see you."

"We were in his room discussing—"

Vehemently, Noriko cuts off my sentence. "Discussing what? I don't believe you, Peter."

She throws herself on the bench seat and bursts into tears. Between sobs, she says, "Why not tell the truth? You have been with some woman, some bargirl."

"No, I haven't." It is surprising how near the truth Noriko often gets.

"You tell a lie."

"I don't."

"Yes, you do."

I lose my temper and quivering with drunken rage I shout, "Shut up! Stop blubbering. Stop being jealous. Shut up and go to bed."

Seething with anger, I storm up the ladder stairs to my room. I long to come down again to clean my teeth and take an aspirin but that would spoil my exit, so I go to bed with a dirty mouth and a throbbing head.

35

I am awakened by Colonel Bogey being played much too adagio, but almost without error. How the girls have improved! Misa-san has a holiday and Kazumi's morning noises and departure for work disturb neither me nor Noriko. I go through the morning fatigues of shaving, washing, dressing, and breakfasting and then I slink back to my bedroom feeling like a malingerer. Noriko is still in bed. At the desk I do nothing but gaze at the temple and think about Noriko, Kazumi, Miss Goto, and my wife. At about ten o'clock, I hear the postman push a letter into a crevice of the front door and I hasten downstairs. My premonition was right. There is a letter from Monica. She is arriving in Tokyo on Saturday and if I do not meet her at the airport, she will assume that I am still in Kyoto and fly here on Sunday; she says she'll stay at the Imperial Hotel in Tokyo and asks me to telephone her there on Sunday morning. What a good thing she doesn't know my Kyoto number! Noriko, if her state of distress does not make her depart today, is due to leave on Sunday. I must see that she takes a morning train for I don't want her to clash with Monica. I shall not tell her about my wife's visit. It is preferable that she hear about it through the post when she is back in Tokyo. Typically, Monica does not say how long she is staying, but then she is not what one would call a letter writer, never committing to paper anything but Olympian statements and imperious commands: "I arrive on the so-and-so. Please meet."

I go back to the bedroom. The girls' rendering of Colonel Bogey now has more brio. At ten-thirty with my heart thumping a bit I go into Noriko's room. She is lying on her back (she always sleeps on her back) with her eyes open; the upper sheet has been kicked back and her diaphanous nightdress is above her knees which are knobbly, and her calves are rather fat. The sun has already invaded the room and it is hot.

"Time to get up," I say, jovially.

She looks at me for a moment and then, spontaneously, it seems, jumps to her feet, throws her arms round my neck, and sobs, "Sorry, darling!"

"It's all right, but you mustn't be silly. I—" I can't bring myself to use the powerful verb "to love," a verb I can only use when tipsy or with someone new. "I am very fond of you, you know. You must realize that."

"Yes, I know. I am very silly. I love you so."

"You'd better get dressed. I thought it'd be nice to have lunch at the Miyako Hotel."

"Oh yes!" Noriko gives me another hug and I have to submit to a long kiss to which I attempt to respond with passion but rather fail to do so.

The rest of the morning goes smoothly. Noriko makes her own breakfast and I sit with her in the dining recess, feet dangling and trying to avoid hers. She washes the dishes, makes my bed, and dusts corners that Misa-san has missed. I suddenly remember the bamboo brooch and fish it out of the drawer in the desk and give it to her as a reward; she is sweetly grateful. If one had wanted a title for the morning, "Conjugal Bliss" or "Harmony in the Home" would have been apt.

Noriko likes going to grand Western-style hotels and when, in order to keep my spirits up I go downstairs to pour myself a large vodka martini, she asks if she should wear a hat.

"No." She has a sort of straw cloche, which may be modern, but in which she looks dreadful. Western hats do not suit Japanese faces; they make them look perky. In old times women in Japan never wore hats. They decorated their hair with tortoiseshell combs and coral-tipped hairpins (there is a smattering of the South Sea Islands about the country) but they did not wear hats, except soup-plate ones for working in the fields.

"Why not?"

"It is too hot for a hat, I should have thought, and besides you look much better without one."

"Do I, darling?" Noriko is pleased that I am talking about her.

"You know I think so. I've said so before. And you couldn't put a hat on top of that hair."

"Do you like this style?"

Her hair is piled on top of her head (in imitation of Kazumi?) and this does not suit her because it leaves uncovered her ears, which are small, round, and lobeless, not elongated and shapely as ears should be. "Oh, yes," I say, lukewarmly.

"*Darling!*" she kneels at my feet and kisses my hand. "I am so happy."

I pat her head.

"Look out my hair!" she laughs and then she rises and sits on my lap.

"Don't spill my drink."

"Sorry, darling."

The telephone rings. Noriko is off my knees and squatting by the phone in a flash.

"It's Miss Goto." From Noriko's expression it might be a telegram announcing a death.

I go to the phone. "Hello, Miss Goto. How good of you to call!"

"You have a student with you? I am sorry to trouble you, Mr. Meadowes. I was hoping . . . I wanted to tell you about the Noh play they are performing at the drama festival on Saturday. It is called *Shunkan*. It is about three men who are banished to an island and—"

"Miss Goto, I am afraid I can't listen to a summary now. I am having a session with some students. You told me yesterday that you had got two tickets, but could you get four tickets? It doesn't matter if they aren't together or in the same row. I have two friends who very much want to come—just a moment, please." I put my hand over the mouthpiece. "Noriko, do you want to go to the drama festival on Saturday?"

"Are you going?" Noriko invariably asks this question, as if I might be planning to get her out of the way.

"Yes."

"Of course I want to go." Noriko always says this.

I speak into the phone. "Yes, four tickets, please, Miss Goto. And could you come to dinner first?" Recklessly, I think it would be amusing to have the three women eating at the same table. I should be able to compare them, or their table manners at least.

"I was hoping," goes on Miss Goto, determinedly, "to come and see you to explain about the Noh play."

As if I haven't heard, I ask, "What time does it begin?"

"At seven p.m."

"Come here at a quarter to six. We'll have an early meal. Good-bye, Miss Goto." I look up. Noriko is wearing the same ugly expression she put on last night. "What's the matter?"

"Why she ring you up every day?"

I sigh. "It's about the drama festival. I told you."

"I think she loves you."

"She may, but I certainly don't love her."

"Are you sure?"

"Oh God, Noriko! We went through all this yesterday." I shout, "I DO NOT LOVE HER. I DO NOT LOVE MISS GOTO. I don't even know her first name. You're as jealous as Juno."

I go into the kitchen and pour myself a stiffer vodka martini.

36

Situated on the side of a hill on the eastern rim of the city, the Miyako Hotel is a massive, hybrid block enlarged several times in several styles and in several directions. Its rambling interior is mostly Western, but the upper heights contain a few Japanese rooms for tourists who want to tell their friends that they have taken off their shoes, sat on their heels at low tables, and slept on tatami. The majestic entrance porch with its uniformed doormen, the spacious lobby with its red-jacketed bellhops and somberly clothed desk clerks are impressive enough to intimidate all but the most hardened of travelers. They do not intimidate me, of course, but they do Noriko, who, on tiptoe with her tongue between her lips, follows me up a flight of stairs and along a passage to the observation lounge. We sit in the window of the huge horseshoe of glass and at once Noriko gets excited about the view, which commands a fair part of the northern section of the city. Perched on the edge of an armchair, she points at the landmarks. "There's the Heian Shrine, there's Nanzenji, there's the Asahi Shinbun building, I think . . ."

I order a large vodka martini and an orange juice. I have often wished that Noriko drank at least an occasional glass of wine, for when I am high on several cocktails, she, after her soft drinks, is in the same cold-sober state as at the beginning of the preprandial bout. While I feel festive, all Noriko feels is hungry. One of the advantages of my wife is that she enjoys having a drink or two; when Monica and I sit down to dinner our minds are racing at the same speed; we are both on the same level of conviviality.

The view is the reason for coming to this lounge, for it gives people who have nothing to say to one another something to talk about. Also, I enjoy Noriko's delight, even though it makes me feel more like an uncle than a lover. If my wife were here (and she almost is!) she would say in her gruff, smoker's voice that carries so disastrously, "God, how squalid! All those wooden huts with gray roofs! The place looks like a rundown mill town in Lancashire. You say that is a temple? It looks like a great cowshed." In a way I prefer Noriko's naive interest to my wife's sophisticated carpings. But do I? I have sometimes thought of taking Noriko on a tour of Europe simply to enjoy the sights through her eyes, and yet I know I should be bored after I had expatiated on the history, architecture, the paintings of Venice, say, or Florence, or Vienna. I should get a ration of that glow of contentment which a teacher has after giving a successful lesson, but it would not last; it would fade with the evening sun and the return to the hotel for my whiskey and her orange juice, because while Noriko would listen, nod, and coo, she would offer nothing: she would not criticize what I had said and I could tell her anything, invent the most fantastic nonsense; she would have nothing to say except "beautiful," "very interesting," "I liked it very much," in reply to my needling "What do you think?" She would be an ignorant and not a very intelligent pupil. But if I took Mrs. Kato, an erudite widow and one who is really knowledgeable about Western art, or if I took Professor Saito, who really understands Shakespeare and would be the most appreciative guest, I would be bored since one needs more than intellectual companionship. To take Mrs. Kato or Professor Saito would be a kindness, one that would never be forgotten. Better to take Noriko, for by taking her I would at least be repaying back her devotion in a way. But no, I shall not take Noriko to Europe, even though she longs to go. She longs to go so much that she buys a lottery ticket every month hoping to win enough money for the trip. I have constantly explained that what with my wife, a child, and a house to keep up (not true, as Monica forks out more than I do for the expenses), I cannot afford to pay for round-the-world jaunts. Meekly, Noriko has accepted this and gone on buying lottery tickets.

"What is that hill over there?" Noriko points.

"Mount Hiei."

"No, the small one, there."

"I don't know. I am going to have another drink, would you like another orange juice?"

"No, thank you. I have had quite sufficient." This means that she is hungry and wants to eat.

I order another drink.

Noriko frowns. She disapproves of my drinking and often says censoriously, "You drink too much. It is bad for your health." The Japanese are pathologically valetudinarian.

"Does that matter to you?" I say.

"Yes it does," Noriko replies, emphatically, "because you are not only yourself." I hate this expression, which is always cropping up in popular songs.

Later, over the lunch table, when half a bottle of claret has mellowed my feelings towards Noriko even more (I do not remove my foot when she places hers on top of mine), Noriko says, "May I ask you a question?"

Preparing myself for a bomb, I answer, "Yes, of course."

"Who is Juno?"

After lunch I want nothing more than to have a siesta, but Noriko wishes to see a temple (when the Japanese get to Kyoto they have an urge to go sightseeing), and feeling indulgent towards her I agree to accompany her to Nanzenji, which is near the Miyako Hotel and not far from my house. We take a taxi to the main, two-storied, double-roofed gate, which stands by itself amidst pines and maples, just inside the wall that encloses the complex of buildings of this Zen institution. It is three o'clock in the afternoon and crushingly hot; however, a slight breeze and the sound of rushing water nearby help. We walk up to the main building, take off our shoes (there are not many other sightseers), and dutifully go round the shiny, wooden corridors looking at the screens in the rooms and stopping for a moment or two to admire the sand and rock garden.

Noriko would have stayed longer, but I have seen the place before and I yearn for my bed. She—the effort of following seems less than that of trying to dissuade her—insists on going up a rough, arbored path at the end of which rises the thickly wooded hill that is Nanzenji's impressive backdrop. Beside the path runs a stone aqueduct which is high up and massive. We pause to gaze at this alien structure, and then we go on up the path and reach the top where the aqueduct meets the ground and turns a corner. I mop my face with my handkerchief, which has become saturated as a dish cloth, and think of the Pont du Gard and Istanbul. We round the corner and a few yards away with their backs towards us is a group of about twenty men, all in summer shirts and slacks and every one of them with a camera. Bunched in a sort of Rugby scrum, they are feverishly focusing and excitedly clicking their apparatuses at something that seems to be on the parapet of the aqueduct, now only a few feet above the ground.

"What are they photographing?" I ask.

Noriko squeezes through the phalanx of men and then comes back to me at the rear.

"A girl," she says.

"A girl?" I reply in surprise.

As if on safari and approaching a much sought-after but feared quarry, and looking between the neat black heads of two very occupied young men, I see an attractive young girl. She is sitting on the parapet and posing. Her face is turned to the side for profile shots and she is gazing at the point where the aqueduct disappears into the hill. I watch, mesmerized. She is so professional: the way she licks her lips to keep her smile fresh, and the way she crosses her legs with just the right amount of knee on display; she is so glamorous: her hair looks as if it had been very recently groomed by an expert, and her face painted by a make-up artist. There is a film star's effulgence about her. The photographers, earnest and serious, point their cameras, click their shutters, turn on their films with the desperateness of fanatical ornithologists who have for the first time seen the rarest bird in the book and are afraid that it will fly away. There is a kind of frenzy about their concentration, and at the same time something lustful.

I rejoin Noriko.

"Who is she?" I ask.

"I don't know. They belong to camera club. She work for camera club posing."

"How ridiculous!"

"It's horrible."

"What?"

"The men."

"Why?"

"They want her."

"All of them?"

"I think yes."

"You mean they're lustful, want sex?"

"Yes."

"They can't all have her, can they?" I say in jest.

But Noriko is serious. "They have her, if they can."

I see what she means. The men resemble rabbits. I wonder why Noriko has had this reaction to the scene. Have her eyes suddenly been opened to the fact that men are animals?

"All men like them," Noriko says, primly. Is this an oblique reference to me?

"Am I?" We are returning to the temple. I look round. The photographers are like bees round their queen.

"Am I?" I repeat.

"Maybe," says Noriko, without smiling. How annoying she can be! However, I do not get cross with her because I have decided to be pleasant, tolerant, and reasonable.

38

It is Saturday, the day of the drama festival and the eve of Noriko's return to Tokyo and my wife's arrival in Kyoto. The two days since our lunch at the Miyako Hotel have passed happily, thanks to my unselfishness. I have behaved considerately, most considerately, taking Noriko to see temples in the day and on excursions at night. I have not referred to the remark she made about those lustful pho-

tographers. On one evening I took her and Kazumi to Mount Hiei
Hotel to see the view and on the other to Arashiyama to watch the
cormorant fishing. At Arashiyama we sat on the floor of one of
those flat-bottomed boats (like the one she and I had hired on her
previous visit), which had paper lanterns hanging from its roof and
was punted by an old man about the river. We watched the cor-
morants being hurled into the water by the grass-skirted fishermen
and in the lights of braziers hanging over the bows of the boats we
saw the birds bob and dive for trout—the fact that this is not serious
fishing but a display laid on for tourists did not trouble us at all. We
bought "boat" fireworks and sent them skimming across the water;
we drank Coca-Cola; we ate rice biscuits; we had a real Japanese
summer evening and I greatly enjoyed it. I wished, though, that I
had been alone in the boat with Kazumi, who more than once
touched my toe with hers when Noriko was looking at the fishermen or a firework.

Kazumi has been maddeningly provocative as she was last time
my "Number One" was here; she has allowed me to give her surreptitious kisses when Noriko has only just been out of the way. This
morning I kissed her in the sitting room when Noriko had her back
turned to us momentarily. It was monstrous of me to do it, but I
couldn't help myself and Kazumi seems to get a thrill out of exciting
me at embarrassing and frustrating moments.

Noriko and I might have been on our honeymoon the way I
have indulged her. Apart from the treats already mentioned I have
allowed her to sleep with me and with my eyes shut and thinking of
Kazumi on the other side of the house I have availed myself of my
master's rights, which Noriko has been only too willing to grant.
And even afterwards I have been tender, behaving like a loving
bridegroom rather than the bored sheik I have really resembled.

This evening at a quarter to six we are having our early meal
before going to the drama festival, and Miss Goto is coming. I have
told Noriko again that my relationship with Miss Goto is merely
that of teacher and pupil and that I have asked her to come because
I want her to explain the Noh play (the Japanese contribution to
the festival), and Noriko has accepted this fiction; she would not be
able to explain the play since she has no knowledge of Noh drama. I
pray that emotional Miss Goto will not give anything away by

throwing herself at my feet and declaring her love or anything silly like that. It is a good thing that Kazumi will also be here for Miss Goto is unlikely to try and pump the girls if they are together. I am relying on that shyness the Japanese have of strangers to silence Miss Goto to whom the epithets brazen or prating could never be applied, or I don't think they could. She was rather brazen in my bedroom, but not until she had switched off the lights.

I rang Bob this morning to see if he could come to the meal, so that the conversation among the women would be even more conventional than usual, for he claims he can understand anything that is said in Japanese, no matter how fast it is spoken.

"Have you forgotten about the play?" he asked, indignantly.

"Indeed not, Bob, but you're not appearing, are you?"

"No, I am not appearing, but I have to be there to see that everything is all right: costumes, make-up, scenery, you know."

"Can't all your assistant directors, stagehands, and so on see to things?"

"No, they can't."

Though Noriko was safely out of earshot in Kazumi's room, I lowered my voice. "I rather wanted your help to balance the females. I have three: Kazumi, Noriko, and Miss Goto."

"Miss Goto! Lord! You're not still mixed up with her, are you?"

"She got the tickets."

"Why not ask Professor Nakayama?"

"The Alice Meynell fan? That's an idea."

"He'd be delighted to come and I know he's very anxious to see my production. So why not invite him?"

"Would he be able to get a ticket?"

"There'll be plenty on sale at the door, if he hasn't already got one."

"Would it be wise to introduce him to my private life?"

"Wouldn't matter. He knows all about my private life. Sometimes he helps to arrange it. We often go out together. Invite him."

"I shall."

Professor Nakayama, who arrives at five-thirty while I am directing Noriko and Kazumi in the kitchen, is younger than he seemed the last time I met him and we went to that bar. I suppose he is about forty. His sleek black hair is beginning to show signs of turning gray, I notice with pleasure, and there is a glint of gold when he smiles. His complexion is florid. He is unshy and readily accepts a whiskey and lights a cigarette. For a few minutes while Kazumi and Noriko are in the kitchen, we discuss his favorite poet, about whom he knows far more than I.

"Which is your favorite poem of Alice Meynell's?" he asks.

"Oh, 'The Lady of the Lambs,' I think." It is the only one I can remember.

"That's in the *Oxford Book of English Verse*," Professor Nakayama says derisively, as if its inclusion in that anthology damned the poet somehow.

"Is it?" I know it is.

"What about her sister's pictures?"

"Er . . ." I have forgotten her artist sister.

"Elizabeth Southerden Thompson who married Sir William Francis Butler in 1877."

"Oh, yes . . ."

"What about her pictures?"

I hazard, "Very nineteenth century."

He gives a little snort. "What about her illustrations of the *Preludes?*"

I have never seen them but I say, "Too pre-Raphaelite for my taste, but I suppose they served their purpose."

At that moment Kazumi comes into the room with a plate of rice biscuits and from that moment Alice Meynell is forgotten. The professor is clearly very taken with Kazumi and she seems to like him, or anyway she likes to flirt, perhaps to tease me. She sits next to the professor on one of the bench seats and lets Noriko complete the culinary preparations; she has taken pains with her appearance and looks quite glamorous. Infuriatingly, and rather rudely, I think, the professor and Kazumi converse in Japanese, thus excluding me from this conversation. Then Miss Goto arrives. Noriko enters the room and I'm not able to watch Kazumi. I have to look after Miss Goto at whom Noriko jerks a brief bow before returning to the kitchen. Miss Goto sits self-effacingly on the very edge of the far end of the other bench seat; she seems to have been struck dumb and so only one-way conversation is possible. Kazumi and the professor are getting on very well, too well for my liking, and I am beginning to feel envious of the attentions she gives the personable expert on Alice Meynell, and it hurts that she has never heard of the poetess and that they are not talking of her.

"What is the name of the Noh play?" I ask Miss Goto.

She does not reply. With bowed head she stares at her lap.

"Miss Goto," I ask, as if coaxing a child, "What is the name of the Noh play?"

"*Shunkan,*" she mutters, and then her chin goes deeper into her chest.

I realize that she is upset at not having me to herself, but I did ask her to get me four tickets and therefore she must have imagined that there would be others in the theater party. Anyway this retreat into extreme diffidence is, I suppose, better than a barefaced denouncement of me, but on the other hand if one arranges a confrontation one perhaps hopes that some sparks will fly.

Noriko enters from the kitchen very much in the manner of the harassed housewife and announces that the meal is ready.

I stand near the telephone and signal Miss Goto to the place opposite me at the end of the table, Kazumi to the one on my right, Noriko to my left, and Professor Nakayama to the place by Noriko. Obstinately, the professor edges round behind Miss Goto and sits next to Kazumi.

Impolitely, I protest, "That place isn't laid."

My objection goes unheeded.

"Never mind," says Kazumi. She reaches across the table for the professor's knife, fork, side plate, and napkin.

"I hope you all like spaghetti," I say, sourly. I am glad I haven't put myself out and provided a proper dinner. "And there's some Bolognese sauce. Noriko, where's the sauce?"

"Oh, I forget!" Noriko leaps up from the table and goes into the kitchen.

"Do you like Bolognese sauce, Miss Goto?"

Miss Goto is gazing at her plate.

Kazumi speaks to her in Japanese and she mumbles "Yes" without looking up.

"Shall I bring the grated cheese, *darling?*" Noriko cries from the kitchen.

"Yes."

Miss Goto starts as if someone had jabbed her with a pin. She gives me a look of deep reproach, and then flicks her eyes down to her plate. I am annoyed with Noriko for breaching Japanese etiquette and using a word of endearment in front of strangers (I know she used it purposely to show that she is on more than familiar terms with me) and sorry for Miss Goto, who is suffering. It was cruel to have arranged for Miss Goto's disillusionment to take place in public, but I didn't consciously plan to do so. Kazumi, Noriko, and Professor Naka-yama eat their spaghetti uninhibitedly, sucking the strands into their mouths, biting off bits, and letting the ends fall back onto their plates. Only now and then does Miss Goto raise her fork to her mouth.

When the spaghetti has all gone, the professor offers round his packet of cigarettes. Kazumi and Noriko take one, while Miss Goto and I refuse.

"Miss Goto and I are the sensible ones," I say, "aren't we, Miss Goto?"

My attempt to be jocular fails and ignoring me and Miss Goto the other three start to talk in Japanese. Miss Goto regards her half-empty plate; the lines of a frown mark her forehead just above the bridge of her rimless glasses. I lightly drum my fingers on the table feeling as out of things as Noriko must have felt when I have been discussing subjects unknown to her in English.

The doorbell rings. Conversation ceases. Miss Goto jumps.

Noriko turns to me. "Who is that, darling?"

"Go and see, will you?"

She hesitates. The bell rings again.

"Go on, Noriko."

"All right, darling." She gets up, slides open the fusuma and after passing into the hall, shuts it again carefully. The front door rattles open. And then there is a voice, an unmistakable contralto that I know only too well.

"Mr. Meadowes?"

I can't hear Noriko's reply, but presently the fusuma shoots open and there stands Monica towering above the table to which I am riveted.

"What on earth are you doing down there?" Monica asks.

"Having supper."

"At this hour?" She looks even more of a giantess than she might have done for she has not taken off her shoes.

"We're going to the theater."

"In this heat?"

39

And then, probably because of nervous shock, I laugh. Monica laughs too, her deep laugh that has never been without a ring of humor. The Japanese at the table glare in amazement. Noriko has regained her place next to me at the table, as if Monica were an apparition that might go away if ignored.

I heave myself off the floor and mumble people's names by way of introduction.

"Monica, I thought it was tomorrow, Sunday, that you were—"

"I got my days muddled. The International Date Line. I thought it worked the other way."

"But how on earth did you find this nameless lane?"

"I rang the British Council and a charming young man came round to my hotel and brought me here in his motor. Wasn't it kind of him?"

"Yes," I say, doubtfully.

"I would have phoned you from Tokyo, where I arrived yesterday, but I didn't have your number."

"Of course," I say, vaguely, "I forgot to give it to you. How silly of me!"

"I must say I take my hat off to the British Council. They're so awfully good at giving you information like an address or something. Do you remember Jack and Betty in Beirut?"

"Jack and Betty!" A host of memories invades my mind. "Would you like to have something to eat, Monica?"

"No, thanks.

"Well, won't you join us?"

"Down there?" she points to the table round which the three women and Professor Nakayama are sitting.

Kazumi and Professor Nakayama are staring wide-eyed at Monica, twisting round to do so, but Miss Goto and Noriko have their eyes down like housewife bingo players at a converted cinema.

"Yes. We haven't had our pudding."

"I don't think I could get down there, Peter. Couldn't I sit in that room?" She jerks her head at the sitting room.

"Yes, do."

Monica sits on one of the bench seats, crosses her legs, and lights a cigarette. She is wearing a white dress with a billowing skirt and full sleeves, which must be rather hot.

I start to rejoin her. Noriko stops me saying, "Don't you want apple?"

Noriko seems less upset than I thought she would be at this her first encounter with my wife; of course Monica has not met her before, knows nothing of her, and Noriko is aware of this.

"Bring me some in there. Monica, would you like some stewed apple?"

"God, no!"

Noriko fusses into the kitchen and I go into the sitting room.

"From your description of the house," Monica says, "I didn't think it was quite 'me.' I cabled the Miyako and that is where I'm staying. Just as well, isn't it?"

I do not take up this obvious reference to the Japanese women. The others, apart from Noriko, are still at the dining table. Kazumi and Professor Nakayama are chatting conspiratorially. Miss Goto, her frown even deeper, her face even whiter, looks as if she might vomit; she is gazing unseeingly into space.

"Have a drink, Monica?"

"What have you got?"

"Most things."

"Any tonic?"

"Yes."

"A vodka and tonic then, *darling*."

For the second time in the same hour I wince at that word; it's as if some devil had put it into my wife's mouth for she rarely uses it to me. Monica looks older, after all she is fifty-four; her hair seems grayer, her face more lined, but being tall she has not lost her figure and she is still a very striking woman. I wonder how old she appears to the Japanese. I go out to the kitchen, where Noriko is dishing out stewed apple. She gives me an accusatory stare, a hurt and reproachful regard.

"I'm sorry, darling. I didn't know she was coming today."

"You know she coming?"

"Yes, but not today."

"You no tell me."

"I didn't want to spoil our nice time together."

"I see. It doesn't matter." Noriko says these words grimly. "Here's some apple for *her*."

"She doesn't want apple. She wants a vodka tonic."

"Vodka!" says Noriko censoriously. "Vodka in the afternoon!" This is an imitation of me when I criticized a friend of mine for drinking at tea time.

"I'm sorry, darling. I do love you, you know."

"I know. I trust you."

Oh God! What a swine I am! I pour out the vodka and Noriko and I leave the kitchen: I with Monica's drink; she with a tray of bowls of apple stew and ice cream. The others have risen from the dining room floor and are sitting in a row on the other bench seat.

Monica is saying, "Alice Meynell? Why on earth her? She's a very minor poet, completely forgotten now."

"I think she's England's greatest poet," says Professor Nakayama, smiling.

"But you can't. She simply isn't. That's all that can be said about it. Christina Rossetti and Emily Brontë were greater poets, weren't they, Peter?"

"What?" I don't want Monica to launch into an attack, though she would only think she was having a discussion.

"Don't you think Christina Rossetti and Emily Brontë were greater poets than Alice Meynell?"

"Emily Brontë, no," I reply. "Christina Rossetti? It's a matter of taste. There should be no best or better in literature." I hastily change the subject. Japanese professors are not good at discussion and I am afraid that Nakayama will be upset, so I say, "How were the Crawfords?"

"Oh, very well. They have the most heavenly house."

I am carried back to the past, the past with my wife. It seems like a previous existence, and, in retrospect, brilliant, much more so probably than it was.

"Have you known my husband long?" Monica asks Noriko in the condescending way she adopts when addressing foreign students.

I interrupt. "The theater! It's time to go. Miss Goto, don't you think we should start?"

Miss Goto says very meekly, "Yes, it is time to go." Her pale face is like a blank sheet of paper.

"Monica, we're going to a drama festival. There's a Noh play, a Kabuki play in English, and a modern Japanese play. I'm sure we could get you a ticket. Would you like to come?"

"I am awfully tired," begins Monica, "but it's too early for bed. Yes, I'll come. I'll come for a bit."

40

We are sitting in the theater, a small modern one which is air conditioned. It is not full. We were able to get Monica a ticket and by asking someone to move up we could all sit in a row. Monica is next to me and Noriko is on my other side; Miss Goto is between Monica and Kazumi, and Professor Nakayama is on Kazumi's right. I would have preferred to have Kazumi next to me, but Noriko was quite determined to sit by me and went into the row first taking my hand and pulling me. "Come along," she said. Her behavior surprises me, as behavior often does in Japan. I don't know if Monica has noticed Noriko's signs of possessive affection towards me. She is observant, so I expect she has and she knows I am inclined to dally.

The Noh play is just over. Throughout it Miss Goto gave a running commentary on what the actors were saying, often leaning across Monica to emphasize a point to me. I wondered if the guide in Miss Goto had conquered her emotions and that the urge to explain was irresistible; or did she still hope to win me by showing her superior knowledge? Kazumi did not once look in my direction. She seemed quite happy to chat with Professor Nakayama. What were they talking about?

"Well, what did you think of it, Monica?" I ask.

"Very strange, but very good. I like the tiny theme."

"And you, Noriko?"

"Very good."

"I presume," says Monica to Miss Goto, "That Shunkan has to remain an exile on the little island for life?"

"Yes," Miss Goto confirms.

"A lesson to you, duckie," says Monica to me.

I make no reply. Surreptitiously, Noriko touches my hand, which I have allowed to dangle down my left side.

"Of course," continues Monica to Miss Goto, "I find the stylized acting very difficult, and the music, the singing. I think I see the point, though. It's like chamber music. Would you agree that in a way it is like a Haydn quartet?"

"Yes," agrees Miss Goto.

"I wish it had been in English. I hate not understanding the words."

"The next play is in English," I say.

"Good," says Monica.

Miss Goto explains, "It is called *Kagotsurube*, which means 'the straw bucket.'"

"Oh, rather a good title," says Monica at once. "Is it a play of disillusionment?"

"The straw bucket is the name of a sword."

"A sword?"

"Yes, for we have a saying that the best sword can cut water."

"Oh yes? But where does the bucket come in?"

"It is the nickname of a sword," goes on Miss Goto.

"But why should a sword be called a bucket?"

It is obviously beyond even Miss Goto to give the reason. She says, "It is just a name."

"It's very peculiar," says Monica to me, but Miss Goto can hear. "I don't understand, but then I never understood much about this country, did I?"

"No," I agree, "but one often has to accept things without knowing the reason for them."

"You, but not I," replies Monica, patly.

The curtain rises on a quarter of the Yoshiwara district in Tokyo. Miss Goto begins her commentary, "The Yoshiwara was the place where men, er . . . it was the pleasure quarter of Edo, old Tokyo."

"Ah, you mean the brothel quarter?" says Monica.

"Really, Monica."

"That is what it is, isn't it?"

"Yes, but—"

"Well, then."

"Shush."

Jiro is talking to his friend. In his shaven-headed wig and kimono Jiro looks fine, but the make-up man has exaggerated his pock marks and painted his face all over with regular round black spots to make it resemble a polka-dot tie. Monica would ask the obvious question: "Whatever's the matter with his face?"

"Smallpox," explains Miss Goto.

"Good heavens!"

"Not really. In the play he has smallpox and—"

I look down the row and see that Bob Watkins is sitting next to Kazumi, and that Professor Nakayama has gone. Was there some sort of plot?

"That's pretty," says Monica when in elaborate kimono and wig Yatsuhashi and a posse of courtesans pass across the stage and pause in front of the amazed Jiro, who, to emphasize the *coup de foudre* he is supposed to undergo at the sight of the beautiful woman, totters about absurdly on his *geta* and falls over.

The audience laugh.

"Is he supposed to be drunk?" asks Monica.

Bob says, "Idiot!"

Miss Goto explains, "He is overcome by the beauty of Yatsuhashi, the grand courtesan."

The curtain descends. The audience clap and laugh. Bob seems very upset by Jiro's accidental fall. "That was not meant," he says down the row to me. "One would think that the boy had never worn *geta* before. Christ!"

The next scene consists mostly of conversation. After a few minutes, Monica says to Miss Goto in a voice I am sure Bob can hear, "What language are they talking in? It doesn't sound like English. I thought you said the second play was in English."

"They are speaking English," replies Miss Goto.

"English? Really?"

Bob scowls.

I am used to the Japanese way of pronouncing my mother tongue and so I know what "Prease cor me" means, but I appreciate that Monica, not used to lambdacisms, cannot understand the request.

Jiro is overacting outrageously. This must be Bob's fault. When Yatsuhashi burns Jiro's hand with the bowl of her pipe, Jiro, instead of simply looked pained, leaps up and jumps about as if a scorpion were biting him.

Monica says, "What's the matter with him now?"

"She burned him with her pipe," explains Miss Goto.

"Thus adding another blemish? What a bitch!"

The laughter that Jiro's cat-on-a-hot-tin-roof act causes upsets the scene completely. Bob scowls again. "Oh God!" he groans. The trouble is that the few native English speakers in the audience can follow the mispronounced dialogue no better than the Japanese, who understand nothing.

Monica, tired from the flight and drowsed by the monotonous and to her incomprehensible dialogue, falls asleep. Noriko, who usually drops off for a while at entertainments, has been away in the land of Nod for some time. I give up the attempt to keep my heavy eyelids from falling and emulate my neighbors.

I awake for the final scene, but the others remain unconscious. Monica is snoring slightly. Miss Goto looks grieved. I notice with alarm that Bob and Kazumi have departed. Can it be that Bob, face lost because of the ghastly performance, has gone off to seek solace with Kazumi somewhere? Damn him! I look at my snoozing wife and then at my snoozing mistress. At least Monica asleep looks intelligent, unlike Noriko who has on her face an expression of benign imbecility. Kazumi's departure with Bob has aroused my anger against her so I sympathize with Jiro, who, having pretended to bring about a reconciliation with Yatsuhashi, suddenly says to her, "My hatred, my levenge, has been glowing daily, but I have hidden it away within me. Today I come for levenge." In spite of replacing the r's with l's, the young man (perhaps Bob's absence makes him less self-conscious) says these lines movingly, and his, "How you

humiliated me!" is said with feeling. He dispatches her quite effec-
tively too. I feel I'd rather like to do the same to Kazumi.

Monica wakes just as Jiro is slaughtering the maid and says, "Ah
sword—you—cut—well!" She is the only member of the audience
to laugh. "Who has he killed?" she asks in an attempt, perhaps, to
smother her mirth.

"The maid," replies Miss Goto.

"Why? What has she done?"

"Maybe she sees him kill the courtesan."

"She's dead too, is she? Oh yes, I see she's lying down. Why did
he kill her? Because she burned his hand?"

"Because she mocked him."

"Well, I can see that that could be a reason for murder."

Jiro is now making his challenging stance, holding his sword
high. He swivels his head, bulges his eyes, screws up his nose, and
beetles his brows. The audience applauds now, for Jiro has not done
this too badly.

Monica laughs. "How absurd!" she exclaims.

"He defies," says Miss Goto.

"How childish!" replies Monica.

41

"So you're still playing with dolls?" Monica
says to me in the taxi just after we have
dropped Noriko at the head of my lane. Miss
Goto hurried off when we left the theater,
refusing a lift. She gave no indication about
how she felt, but Noriko did in a way. Noriko
managed to squeeze my hand and do her blink-wink behind Monica's back as we were getting into the taxi. I took these signals to be
conspiratorial and I understood them to mean that she appreciated
my predicament over my wife's arrival and was prepared to be reasonable, obedient and not create a scene. I am touched by Noriko's
self-restraint and sensible behavior. There is a lot to be said for her
after all. As for Kazumi, she's a bitch. But damn it, fascinating. Is she
with Bob in her flat or an *abekku* hotel?

I do not reply to Monica's sarcasm, but she adds, "That girl's in love with you. I can see that. Are you in love with her?"

"No."

"That makes it easier."

I refrain from asking what Monica means by this statement and banalities pass between us until we are ensconced in armchairs in the bar of the Miyako Hotel. Then Monica says, "That professor would go on about Alice Meynell, of all people, I ask you."

"He's studying her."

"Who ever heard of anyone—"

"Oh, there are plenty of people. You'd be surprised. Anyway Alice Meynell is a good idea. She's sufficiently unknown in Japan for a study of her to be noticed. Shelley and Co. have been overdone. It's rather sensible of him really and I—"

"Sensible! Really, Peter. You know perfectly well that his thesis will be about Alice Meynell's use of the adjective or something futile like that, and getting it all wrong too."

"You underestimate him and Japanese scholarship. Vodka tonic?" I beckon a waiter. He hastens to my side (how wonderful the service is in good hotels in Japan!) and I order Monica's drink and a whiskey for myself.

Monica brings up our daughter and we fall into a chat about her, mutual friends, the house in Suffolk, and I think nostalgically of England and ask myself what I am doing so far away. Monica is right. My daughter needs me, but so does Noriko. Where do my obligations lie?

"You must come back to England with me," says Monica.

I knew before she arrived, of course, that this was her plan.

"But I can't go back now. My contract doesn't expire until March."

"Resign. Say your mother's dying. They don't know she's dead, do they?"

"I suppose not."

My mother, who died four years ago, never liked Monica, but being devoutly religious she disapproved of divorce and even of our living apart; she believed that one should lie in the bed one has made and in no other; also, she thought Monica was to blame for our separation—if she had known the truth! But mothers often refuse to believe the truth about their sons even when they know it.

"Where shall we dine?" asks Monica. "Oh, I forgot, you've dined already. What were you having when I came in? I didn't notice."

"Spaghetti."

"Spaghetti! That hut! Whatever's come over you?"

"Nothing. I happen to like that hut as you call it, and spaghetti Bolognese is one of my favorite dishes."

"It never used to be. Do you remember that house in the Lebanon?"

"Of course."

"I was thinking of it the other day. The Crawfords' house in California reminded me of it. Wasn't the view heavenly!"

I say nothing.

She goes on, "There's no view from that hut you're staying in except onto nondescript shrubbery."

"A tree, a shrub can be as much a view as a bay, green hills."

"What nonsense! It's time you gave up Japan and its myopic mentality." Monica yawns. "I must go to bed. I feel as if I'd been up for a week. I'll get something sent up to my room."

"I'll come round tomorrow."

"Not before noon, please."

"Good night." I peck Monica's cheek and leave. I wonder how much she suspects. I sense she guesses pretty accurately about the part of my life I don't mention to her and I like her for only making a passing reference to it as she did this evening. I walk back to my lane. Noriko is asleep on one of the bench seats. She has not undressed. I know she has been waiting up for me, but I do not disturb her. However when I wake a few hours later, I find her by my side. I move an arm. She turns towards me and puts her right arm round me and hugs. I cannot resist a naked body pressed up against me in the middle of the night, so I make love to her, roll over, and fall satisfied into the arms of Morpheus.

I wonder if Noriko was feigning sleep when I came in.

This is my last but one morning in this house in Kyoto. I am not meeting Monica until noon so I have the morning free to spend with Noriko and to take her to the station. Noriko has been a bit lachrymose. Kazumi has done one of her disappearing tricks. Has she been with Bob? I'm hoping that she'll come back tonight, my last night ever in Kyoto. Monica and I are going to Tokyo tomorrow. I have not told Noriko but I have decided to resign and wind up my affairs. I came to this decision after tremendous exhortations by Monica, who, among a host of things, mentioned my neglect of my paternal duties ("Your daughter is now of an age when she needs a father, not an absentee one, who has opted out," she said); Monica pulled out all the stops. I shall tell Noriko that I can't see her while my wife is with me and that I shall get in touch as soon as she has gone. From Hong Kong, where, no doubt, we'll stay for Monica to do some shopping, I'll write and explain and also offer an allowance. It is better to lie and avoid a scene than to go through all the accusations, screamings, sobbings that the truth might unleash.

At this moment Noriko's little traveling case is in the *genkan*, and she has just come up to my bedroom, where as usual I am sitting at the desk.

"Darling!" Noriko kisses me and the dam starts to leak.

"Now, Noriko, you promised not to cry any more. It is so silly. In a week or so Monica will have left—I told you she was only on a world trip—and everything will be as it has been these last two days in Kyoto. You can come and live in my flat in Tokyo, if you like."

"Are you sure? Do you promise?"

"Of course."

"Maybe you tell a lie."

"Noriko!" I say reprimandingly.

"Sorry."

I don't think she has divined the truth, but also I don't think she believes in a happy ending with me. Time often hangs heavy during the before-leaving-for-the-station period and this morning the weight of the creeping minutes is unbearable. Noriko is by my chair. I gaze into the temple yard and she says, "What are you looking at, darling?" I pick up my nail file, twiddle it in my fingers, and she says, "Do you want me to cut your nails, darling?"

"No, thank you." I put down the file and leaf through Roget's *Thesaurus* and she says, "Is that a good book, darling?" These childish irritances show she's in love but they don't really soften my heart much; indifference might.

I get up.

"Where are you going, darling?"

"To telephone."

"Monica?"

"No, Bob."

"Why?"

"I want to find out why he left the play in the middle."

"Must you do it now? We have only a little time left."

"He may go out." Of course I needn't ring Bob now, but I am burning to know where Kazumi is.

I descend to the sitting room, lower myself on to the floor, and dial Bob's number. He answers after half a ring.

"It's me, Peter."

"Oh, hello there!" Bob sounds rather cool.

"What happened to you? I looked down the row at the end of the play and you'd gone, and so had Kazumi."

"She was feeling unwell. I had to take her home."

"I'm sorry to hear that, Bob. Where is she now? She's not here."

"I took her to her apartment, left her there. It was a nuisance, but what else could I do? You couldn't have taken her home with all those other women in your care."

"Professor Nakayama could have done."

"He'd left. He had some business, so he said."

"So you didn't see the end of the play?"

"No. When I got back to the theater you'd all gone. The place was closing anyway."

So Bob did not return until after the end of the Japanese drama, which must have lasted at least two hours.

"I thought your players improved. The young man did the final scene rather well. Pity you didn't see it."

"So you saw the end?"

"Of course. We left after your Kabuki play."

"When I had to take Kazumi out, you, your wife, and that Japanese girlfriend of yours were fast asleep."

So Bob took the opportunity our dozing gave him to slip out.

"I may have shut my eyes for a while."

Bob grunts.

"Noriko is leaving soon and my wife and I will return to Tokyo, probably tomorrow, so if I don't see you—"

"Well, I'm glad you enjoyed the end of the play," says Bob, a bit sarcastically. "I won't do another Kabuki play again. It's too difficult. It's too Japanese to do in English. In English it's all wrong somehow."

"Sorry not to see you before I go."

"Come down again. It's been nice having you in Kyoto," Bob says in a friendly tone, but it's hard to gauge his feelings. He may be being polite in the Japanese way. I ring off, wondering whether he did spend the afternoon with Kazumi in her apartment. I have a suspicion that he did, but no proof.

Noriko, who has been standing by me, says, "Why did you ask about Kazumi? Always you say, Kazumi, Kazumi."

"I wanted to know what happened to her. You do too, don't you?"

"No."

"Don't you want to say goodbye to her?"

"Not so much."

"Don't you like her?"

"Not so very."

"I thought you did. You seemed to get on well with her."

"Only we talk. I do not like her so very much."

"But why then . . ." I stop. I was going to ask why she chatted with her so merrily, but I know it's no good for I'll never get a proper explanation. I suppose it was all just Japanese politeness or a sort of infatuation that quickly wore off; perhaps she disapproved of Kazumi's flirting with Professor Nakayama, but then she should have welcomed this as she thought that I liked Kazumi. Oh dear, I shall never know exactly what goes on in her mind! I feel I do know how Monica's mind works, though.

By the time we have reached the station, I have begun to have pangs of remorse, and there is a genuine lump in my throat while Noriko and I wait on the platform for the blue-and-white, bullet-nosed, streamlined, air-conditioned super-express. And when the train arrives and I watch her push onto it with the other passengers and then through the sealed window I see her searching for her seat, my eyes fill with tears. Fortunately, the express only stops for two minutes at Kyoto Station, and Noriko only just has time to give me one worried look and a tiny hand-flap before the train moves off. If at this moment, now, I were offered a magic wand which could stop the train, extricate Noriko, and send my wife to Hades, I would wave it furiously.

 I spent the rest of the day showing Monica a few temples. I enjoyed her intelligent appreciation; the gardens particularly interested her since she is a keen gardener herself. Noriko likes the temples but in a different way: she feels their beauty, while my wife's approach is intellectual. I have more in common with Monica's way, the Western way. After seeing a dramatic version of *Finnegan's Wake* given by an American company in Tokyo some years ago, Noriko said she liked it. I thought her praise ludicrous. "But how could you like it when you haven't read a word of Joyce and you hardly understood one sentence?" I asked. "I can feel," she replied. I prefer Monica's logical, cerebral attitude because it is the same as mine. We, Monica and I, want to understand, to know how things work (how a roof is supported, why trees and shrubs in a garden are planted as they are), but Noriko is content to accept the general effect. I don't say that our way is better but I prefer it because I can understand it.

Monica and I dined at the Miyako Hotel and then I left her, ostensibly to complete my packing; in reality I was aching to get back to the house to see if Kazumi had returned. No offer came from Monica to help me pack and she turned down my suggestion (I knew she would) that she might like to move in with me, saying, "No, duckie, I prefer the Miyako." Perhaps she suspects that there is someone I have to disentangle myself from for we did drop Noriko off at the house on the way back from the theater yesterday, and Monica tactfully leaves me to do it without her. She doesn't care about the cost of the Miyako. She has always said, "I'll pay" if I have warned her about something being expensive. That is one of the advantages and at the same time the disadvantages of our marriage: she has always been able to say, "If you can't afford it, I can; and what's more, I shall." This time her superior wealth has worked to my advantage.

I get back from the Miyako Hotel to find Kazumi on the bench seat in her briefs. She is watching television. A young man by the name of Kenji Sawada in a leather jumpsuit open to the waist is bawling about someone called Jennie and waving a pistol in his hand.

"Are you all right, Kazumi-san?"

"Yes." She seems surprised at my question. "Has Noriko gone?"

"I took her to the station this morning. But are you better? Bob said you were ill."

"Oh, yes. I always get claustrophobia in theaters. I feel I must run out. Professor Watkins kindly took me to my *apato*."

"It was good of him, for it meant his not seeing the rest of his play."

"He is very kind." She turns her eyes on to a commercial. A couple seems to be sitting on the Thames Embankment and drinking Nescafé. The Houses of Parliament are in the background. "All the world over, Nescafé," sings a female voice. Kazumi must have seen the advertisement a hundred times. How can it mesmerize her?

"I'm leaving tomorrow," I say. "I'm going with my wife to Tokyo."

"And then?" asks Kazumi.

"I think I shall resign and go back to England."

"And Noriko?"

"I hope she won't copy Cho-Cho-san."

"She may."

I go over to Kazumi. This is my last chance with her. I put a hand on her shoulder. "Kazumi," I say, coaxingly.

She moves, freeing her shoulder. "Please change the channel," she says.

I go over to the TV set and turn the switch. We see a teacher giving a math lesson.

"Change!" Kazumi commands.

Then come girls playing volley ball.

"Change!" Then there is a program I've seen before. It is called *Panchide Deito*, which means "Punch-card Date" and consists of two comedians interrogating alternately a boy and a girl with a view to their becoming engaged. The couple have not met before. At the end the two talk to each other for a few seconds and then, if they click, press a button and a big heart behind them lights up and pulsates. Kazumi loves this absurd program. She finds it romantic. Sometimes one of the pair does not push the button and only half the heart lights up. This happens now. The young man, a student, has been rejected.

"Good," says Kazumi. "I wouldn't want him."

A fresh couple is introduced.

"I'm going to bed," I say.

"Goodni'."

"I shall be gone tomorrow." This has no effect whatsoever, so I go up to my bedroom.

I lie in bed with might-have-been thoughts, going over the last six weeks. Why did Kazumi spurn me? And why did she kiss me only when Noriko was here? Does she get an especial thrill about leading people on and then evading them? A Tantalus woman. Perhaps unfulfillment was for the better; because of it I shall remember Kazumi with desire, whereas if she had become my mistress I might well have been bored with her by now and be going through that awkward end-of-affair period; she might have become like Miss Goto, whom carnal knowledge, even though incomplete, made undesirable. Pity is the emotion that Noriko will arouse in me in the future, pity and shame.

My dozing is disturbed by the temple clappers. I have heard them on and off for almost two months and have got used to them, just as I have grown accustomed to the tree crickets and the bean-curd man's horn. I get up and look out of the window. I see an old woman with a pair of clappers. So the clappers are to warn the inhabitants to be careful about their fires and to lock their doors and not for accompanying late-night prayers. How easy it is for a foreigner to be wrong about this country! I suppose the householders of the street take turns to do this task. I have not been asked to do my stint. Foreigners are not regarded as members of the community, even though they pay taxes.

It is quite cool at five-thirty when I stir, the air having an autumnal freshness. I pull a blanket up from the bottom of the bed and go to sleep again. I wake much refreshed from my second sleep and glancing at the bedside clock I am surprised to see that it is as late as nine-thirty. None of the usual matutinal noises—the slamming of the refrigerator door, the running of the kitchen taps, the flushing of the lavatory—are going on so I presume that either Kazumi is still asleep or that she has gone to work. I stay in bed listening for her descent on the other side of the wall behind my head and as no sound comes I get up, put on my pajama top, and go downstairs. Her shoes are not in the *genkan*, so she must have gone out. However, in order to be sure, I cross the sitting room, turn on the light in the passage, and ascend her steeper stairs, cautiously, one by one, since, alas, I'm not used to them. When I am halfway up I can see through the open door on to her futon, a wide one that covers most of the floor, but the top sheet has been thrown aside. She has definitely gone to work. She might have awakened me to say goodbye. Perhaps she didn't like to, or didn't want to. I complete my climb and enter her room. It is in disorder. Bedclothes, blouses, slacks, skirts hang from the ledge above the window. In a corner, thrown aside, are her briefs. I regard them with envy. How I would have loved to rip them off! Just as I am bending to pick them up the girls' band starts up with Colonel Bogey. The corny march stops me from committing a morbidly sentimental act. For the first time I am grateful to the asinine tune, which makes me think of the rude words that British soldiers used to sing to it and pulls me to my senses. I return to my part of the house, make myself breakfast, and put the final touches to my packing, accompanied by the military music blaring across the street. The girls are surpassing themselves this morning and have launched with confidence into another air. Misa-san the maid, my Cambridge landlady, arrives, puffs up the stairs, and fusses and protests over the fact that I am leaving. I pay her, adding a liberal tip which she refuses twice, then accepts, and puffs down the stairs to the kitchen, where she begins to clatter crockery.

I sit with the fan playing on my back. The bean-curd man is sounding his musical horn; two cicadas on the paulownia tree are screaming; in Higashiyama-dori the diesel engines are throbbing. It is just like any other morning except that the desk is clear of my debris, the girls' band is playing perfectly, and in five minutes I shall be gone.

The person uppermost in my mind is, I am ashamed to say, Kazumi, not Noriko who loves me, not Miss Goto, whom I've hurt. And Kazumi is, I'm sure, not thinking about me at all, but about Bob Watkins, Oliver, Professor Nakayama, Mr. Ohno, Sabu-chan, or more probably, about herself. In any case whenever I hear Colonel Bogey in the future, it won't sound quite the same.

44

Monica and I are in Hong Kong. Friends, who have gone on leave, have lent us their flat, which overlooks the typhoon shelter, the yacht club, and right across the harbor to Kowloon. While Monica goes shopping I stare out of the window at the ships leaving and entering the port; it is easy to read the names of the vessels with my Japanese binoculars. I have become engrossed in the shipping. The *South China Morning Post* publishes a shipping supplement and so I am able to tell whence the ships have come and whither they are going.

I am sitting at a desk as I used to in Kyoto with my papers about Li Ho in front of me, but I have hardly written a line this morning or on any other morning since our arrival a week ago. I look up and a cargo ship flying the Rising Sun flag is leaving the harbor. I take up my binoculars. The ship is the *Atsuta Maru* and, the paper informs me, she is bound for Kobe. I can see an officer in white standing in the bow. He will be in Kobe in five days. The ship becomes partly hidden by the yacht club and then slowly it emerges. Kyoto is just over an hour away from Kobe by express train. I wonder if Kazumi is

still in the house or whether she has gone back to her apartment. I
expect she is in the house. Does Bob Watkins or Professor Nakayama visit her every night and do they lie on my bed with the curtains drawn and the fan playing up and down their naked bodies? A
sailor walks along the deck to the stern and pulls down the flag.
Shouldn't he have waited until the *Atsuta Maru* was properly out of
the harbor? Perhaps the act of taking down the flag makes him and
his shipmates feel farther on in their voyage and nearer their homes.

Kazumi is not worth my thoughts; Noriko is, though. Noriko is
the only person in the world, now that all my close relations are
dead, who remembers my birthday. Monica never remembers it. Last
year Noriko gave me a tie which she had embroidered herself in a
single hem stitch. It is an awful color (the background is tomato and
the embroidery mustard) and I have never worn it, but not having
the heart to throw it away, it is still in my tie collection and I look at
it often; I looked at it this morning as a matter of fact. I have not
written to Noriko yet: I can't bring myself to. She must be wondering why I haven't phoned her from outside my flat. I forbade her to
phone me. I wish I were on the *Atsuta Maru* going back to Japan. I
could fly to Tokyo this afternoon—there are God knows how many
flights a day from Hong Kong—shall I? I wonder for the five thou-
sandth time since I left Japan whether Noriko realizes I have gone. I
departed as planned without letting her know. It is perfectly feasible
for me to be in Tokyo tonight. The plane would probably not arrive
till late, but I could go round to her room. I know exactly where she
lives for I have been there several times. I can see myself now walking through the labyrinth of lanes from Kichijoji Station in the sub-
urbs to her apartment house.

Her *apato* is a six-mat room on the ground floor, which faces
north and has a damp patch on the wall. In it are all the things I
have given her: a record player, a television set, a gas heater, a
bathrobe I was going to throw away, the photographs of England
from an old *Times* calendar, my photograph, and in a cupboard are
all the programs of not only all the operas, ballets, plays, and con-
certs we have seen together, but of all the films too—("You don't
want a program. It's only a film." "I want one." "Why?" "As a memory." "God!"); there is a box containing all the letters I ever wrote
her—("You should burn those." "Never!"); there is an album in

which are stuck the stubs of the tickets for the theaters and the cinemas and the bills from restaurants where we ate together—("That's why you asked for the tickets and the bills. Why on earth do you keep them?" "They are important to me."). I could easily tell her the truth, tell her of her constant loyalty and devotion, tell her that she is the only one who deserves my love and the only one who will have it in the future. Shall I do this?

I realize, though, that if I went back I should be bored with her and hanker after Kazumi or someone like her. Noriko is the Japan I understand, the Japan that I find honest but dull, sweet but plain; Kazumi is the Japan that will always fascinate me, the Japan I shall never know.